Acknowledgments

I thank my God with every remembrance of you...

A nail-scarred hand was extended. An offer of salvation was made. At the joining of my hand and heart to His, my life began anew. With promises of love, acceptance, and faithfulness, Jesus captured me as He turned my mourning into dancing. He became my Ishi, my husband, and a Father to the fatherless. And to Jesus I am eternally grateful.

To my precious and wonderful sons, Ryan and Zach—I thank my God for you. You have been such a blessing and you taught me to smile while I danced, even when times were hard.

As my life continued, God graciously allowed Roger to cut in on the dance and to become my beloved marriage partner. Roger—your support, encouragement, and love so resembled Jesus' own; I never felt a partner change at all. To you Roger, I offer my appreciation and love for being a man of God with integrity with whom my heart and the hearts of our sons were safe. Now as Mimi and Papa to our grandchildren, Avery and Cameron, our hearts dance with delight. It is our joint prayer they become true worshipers of Jesus and dance closer with Him than we have ever known.

To Ginger, the daughter God gave us—thank you for dancing with Avery and loving her Daddy so well.

To my sisters, Carol and Cathy, and my brother, Rick, and my parents now deceased—I thank you all for listening to my long stories at the dinner table when I was young, which gave me practice to write this book!

To Pastor Roger and Beth Bourgeois and my family at Fellowship of Living Praise—you have shown me God's truth through the teaching of His Word and by your daily examples of worship and service to Jesus. I thank you for teaching me the dance steps of commitment and faith and how to follow the lead of the Holy Spirit. You have been used mightily by God in my life, and I appreciate your prayers for me and my family throughout the years.

With a divine sweep, the Lord gathered to Himself a company of dancers with whom I have been proudly associated. The Fellowship of Living Praise Dance Ministry Team exemplifies the dancing Bride of Christ like none other. This book is filled with nuggets of truth He has shown us, and I know you will recognize them. Thank you all for your support, encouragement, and prayers, but especially for being my friends. Dancing with Jesus with you all has been a great honor and blessing. We have cried, prayed, laughed, learned, and worked together as sisters. I believe our greatest dance is yet to come as we dance for the day!

Dancing with
JESUS

Dancing with
JESUS

A NOVEL

LINDA FITZPATRICK

DESTINY IMAGE® PUBLISHERS, INC.

P.O. Box 310, Shippensburg, PA 17257-0310

"Promoting Inspired Lives."

This book and all other Destiny Image, Revival Press, MercyPlace, Fresh Bread, Destiny Image Fiction, and Treasure House books are available at Christian bookstores and distributors worldwide.

For a U.S. bookstore nearest you, call 1-800-722-6774.

For more information on foreign distributors, call 717-532-3040.

Reach us on the Internet: www.destinyimage.com.

ISBN 13 TP: 978-0-7684-4053-9

ISBN 13 Ebook: 978-0-7684-8885-2

For Worldwide Distribution, Printed in the U.S.A.

1 2 3 4 5 6 7 8 / 16 15 14 13 12

Dedication

Revelation 1:19 says, *"Therefore write the things which you have seen, and the things which are, and the things which will take place after these things."* (NASB)

The call to write this book was also heard by my husband, Roger. His support, sacrifice, prayers, and encouragement were invaluable. We join our hands together and now lift this book up in dedication to Jesus. We pray for those who will find a relationship with Jesus and for those who will seek their destiny and purpose in Him as a result of this writing. Dancing with Jesus is glorious!

*"Let them praise His name
with dancing…"* (Psalm 149:3).

Contents

Foreword

The most common question I have received from Christians over the past 32 years as a pastor has been, "What is God's will for my life?" I have been privileged to minister among various expressions of Christianity and in a few foreign nations. The denominational, cultural, or even ethnic expression of Christianity makes no difference. Once the assurance and excitement of being "born again" is settled, the quest of the newly redeemed normally begins focusing on "What now?" Or, "What do I do for God after all that He has done for me? Yes, I'm eternally saved, but what is the purpose of the rest of my life? How can I make a difference in this world? How do I impact my world for the purposes of the Kingdom of God?"

While you may be unfamiliar with this author, I have known Linda Fitzpatrick through life's many ups and downs: the tragic death of her first husband, her solitary years of raising two sons, her new identity as a valued bride to her current husband, and her heartfelt discovery of her divine identity and destiny in

Jesus. I have not only witnessed her personal quest to come into alignment with Father's will and desire for her life, but I have personally traveled this path with her.

This book is about a young lady named Abia whose divine purpose and identity were established before the foundations of the earth were established, and yet the enemy of all of God's children attempted to steal, kill, and destroy Father's will for her life. That's what satan does! He attempts to abort Father's divine destiny and identity for His children. That's all satan can do because there is no truth, no life, and no creativity in him. However, the book doesn't stop there; it is also an intriguing story of one's divine calling, ensuing disappointment, marvelous redemption, strong character, deep revelation, and realization of satisfying spiritual fulfillment. This story is about receiving the unfolding fulfillment of God's best! The quest is completed when the Holy Spirit propels, empowers, teaches, and directs the servant of Christ how to personally express the presence of the Father in the Kingdom He is establishing on the earth. Abia comes into the full knowledge of how to please her heavenly Father!

This is truly a quest that Linda Fitzpatrick has personally experienced. It is Linda's own redemptive story that unfolds before the reader. A tragic accident seemingly aborted Linda's own destiny to become a dancer. However, her personal encounters with Jesus first healed her spirit and then her body, enabling her to fulfill her Kingdom destiny with power and purpose. She not only understands the power of dance for either evil or good, but she also understands the sheer joy of pleasing the Lord of the Dance!

Let me issue a friendly warning to the reader. This story will captivate you. You will be compelled to read the next chapter, then the next. You will not want to put this book down once you begin to read it! It will draw you into the setting and characters like Elijah was swept up into a whirlwind. The dramatic blend of the main character's growing spiritual life in a combination of both the historical and spiritual worlds will keep you desiring more as you move from one adventurous chapter to the next. Even the conclusion will leave you desirous of a sequel. You will be asking, "Where does Abia go from here? I want to know more; tell me what happens to her now that she has discovered Father's will for her life!"

Roger Bourgeois
Pastor

Prologue

"Hannah?" Yaron Ben-David questioned sleepily while feeling the warm indention in the bed beside him where his wife had been. His bare feet searched the floor for his sandals, but not before discovering that the late summer's sun that made the town of Jerusalem in the year of 3778 hot by day had long since turned the dirt floor cool by night. Still trying to find his shoes, his feet made sleepy circles while he rubbed the remaining slumber from his eyes.

A small, ruddy, clay olive oil lamp produced a soft golden glow that framed the face of his lovely wife, giving away her location and just enough light to provide a clue to his missing right sandal. Standing in the narrow doorway, Yaron observed a scene he had never grown tired of seeing in the 17 years of their marriage: his faithful wife with his wonderful children who were sleeping safe and sound nearby. That could not be said of many Jewish families of the region, nor of his own family of origin.

Allowing himself a brief visit to the earlier days of his childhood, he recalled that the then 17-year-old Yaron's life had been an ordinary one. He had lived a peaceful life next to the shores of Galilee with his father, who was busied by the daily chores and hard work of being a fisherman, his mother, and his 2-year-old brother—until the day when the Roman soldiers stormed Bethlehem and all its vicinity in search of a young child whose birth enraged King Herod.

Magi, or wise men, from a different part of the world had seen a new star in the heavens, which was a sign to them of the arrival of a new King. Being led to this region, the Magi made inquiries of King Herod as to the whereabouts of the newly born King of the Jews. King Herod held an unreasonable fear of anyone he considered a threat to the kingdom of Judah, and he gave the command to his soldiers to find the child with the pretense of worshiping Him. When the child could not be found, in an obsessive fit of rage Herod commanded all male children around two years of age in Bethlehem, and surrounding towns and villages, to be slaughtered. Each house was violated as the soldiers searched for little boys to be slain.

The screaming refrain could be heard down every street and from every home, including his own. Pushing Yaron aside, they scanned the darkened room in search of their prey. His father's strong body made a temporary shelter, but the two bloodthirsty soldiers knocked him to the ground, only to reveal his mother and baby brother. Their pleading fell on deafened ears as one of the soldiers jerked from his mother's arms the youngest son of Ben-David. With one slice, his brother's innocent blood left yet another stain on the soldier's uniform as they quickly turned their attention to finding more victims. His family's horrified screams joined the growing chorus of voices from Jewish families throughout history as another tragic stanza was written.

With a quick shake of his head, Yaron tried to bring his thoughts to the present and once again scatter the horrendous memories of the past. As he peered into the adjoining room, gratitude filled his heart. Although he could not understand the ways of God, he was thankful to be alive.

God had indeed blessed him once again with a wonderful family and flourishing sewing business, for which he was eternally thankful. The modest rectangular house on the end of a street not far from the open market in Jerusalem provided adequate space for them all. It joined other houses around a central shared courtyard where water was gathered daily from the public well and stored in the courtyard cistern. Their house had three rooms that made an "L" shape, with the bigger room in the center and two small rooms flanking each side. Inside the largest room was a set of stairs that led to the flat roof of their house.

The larger room, which they called the kitchen room, was utilized in a variety of ways. It was large enough so that giant bolts of thick fabric, used for making boat sails, could be billowed out to be sewn on wooden tables. Large black cooking pots of boiling water and dyes were in the corner of the kitchen. They were used for dying fabrics different colors, as requested by their clients when they placed their orders. The kitchen room was the coziest room in the house in the winter, but was extremely hot in the summer. When the heat became too oppressive, they moved the pots outside into the courtyard if weather permitted. It was a fully functional kitchen as well, but at night it doubled as a bedroom for his son. To the right of the larger room was the bedroom Yaron shared with his wife. The smaller room on the left housed his two daughters.

Stepping out in search of his wife, he almost tripped over the long legs and growing feet of their 13-year-old son, Samuel. The blanketed pallet, which was no longer sufficient for the young man's growing body, was in the hallway just outside the kitchen in an attempt to escape the still smoldering ashes beneath the black pots. As he looked down at his son, he was once again filled with gratitude. He knew firsthand how valuable sons were when he alone had to do a greater share of the work after the death of his own brother. *A son and such a hardworking boy*, he thought to himself proudly, as did all good Jewish men with their firstborn sons. "Samuel the Dependable" had been true to the nickname given to him as he worked so diligently as a young child when the family business first began. Careful not to step on his son, Yaron went to his daughters' room. The mere thought of them brought a smile to his sleepy face.

Abia, his five-year-old daughter, and Judith, his three-year old, slept together on a small blanketed mat in the corner of the small room. All the babies had first slept in their parents' room, but when the next was born, the small room became theirs. Samuel had the room to himself for ten long years before Abia came along. After Judith was born and became old enough to sleep away from her parents, she and Abia shared Samuel's room, forcing him to sleep in the kitchen room. Samuel was as taken by his sisters as their father, and the sacrifice was made gladly.

Abia and Judith were Yaron's pride and joy. They could always make him laugh, and their sweet innocence pulled at his heartstrings. *Just like their mother, Hannah*, he recalled as he compared the three wonderful females in his life. Sharing long, dark auburn hair; soft, upturned smiles; and almond-shaped, brown eyes, each possessed a power over him of which they never took full advantage. They loved to sing and dance, making a loving and lively home for him to live in.

Still in her wheat-colored tunic undergarment, Hannah cradled Abia, whose body shook from tears brought on by a dream. "Hush, little one, it was only a dream," she whispered, trying not to awaken the round ball of Judith nuzzled beside her and Samuel, who was sleeping in the hall nearby.

"He let go of my hand, Momma," Abia's pink lips formed a drowsy pout as she gave reason for the tears.

"Who let go of your hand, Abia?" Hannah inquired, thinking of her husband's strong, sun-weathered hands or Samuel's lanky ones.

"Oh, Momma, He is the nicest man in the whole, wide world..." she stopped as she saw her Papa approach.

"Is that so, little Abia?" Papa said teasingly, as if he were a little jealous of the other man's compliment. With his large hand he gently removed from her peach-colored cheek a wisp of dark brown hair.

"Oh, Papa, you know you are the most handsome!" she said with a sleepy grin.

"Go back to sleep, my little sweet-talker!" His heart was warmed by the flattery and the love that escaped through her playful but sleepy eyes.

"Yes, Papa," she obeyed him at the same time that she finished her sentence.

With the Ben-David family nicely settled back into their beds, Hannah took advantage of having some quiet time with her husband. Although they worked together side by side stitching and producing other merchandise, she had very little opportunity to speak to him without the interruption of daily life routines and children.

"Yaron, do you remember last year when Abia started to have unusual dreams?" she asked in a whisper to keep the children from hearing.

"Yes, I remember," he responded in the same quiet tone. "She talked of a man in her dreams who loved to see her dance," he said with a protective air. "At first, I was quite alarmed, but it was all very innocent. It always made Abia quite happy when He was in one of her dreams. He told Abia she was greatly treasured by God and was created to dance for Him. He instructed her to dance and twirl with delight every time she thought of God."

Hannah nodded in agreement. "One afternoon I found her playing outside with Judith. Abia was humming a tune I had never heard before. She was also talking with little Judith in a language I had never before heard. When I asked her where she had learned it, she told me the man in her dreams had taught it to her, and whenever she wanted to be near God, she could speak and sing to Him as she danced."

"A few months ago I was giving her a bath one evening when she told me of another dream she had," Hannah recalled. "In this dream, she was walking with the man down the street market in Jerusalem. As they traveled down the street, people were coming up to the man, and as they did, He healed them. He healed them of all types of 'hurts' she called them. Excitedly she told me again how good the man was to do such kind things for the people. But that was not the entire dream. The man said she could be His helper and do good things for people, too. As they walked down the street together, they spoke to each other in the strange language. Whenever she heard Him make a certain sound, she danced, and as she danced, the people they passed along the street were healed!"

Both father and mother were very confused in the attempt to make sense of their little daughter's dreams.

"When another month passed, Abia had another dream and this one was not a happy one like the others had been," Hannah told her husband. "This one made her very upset, causing her to cry uncontrollably. Not like this evening when she cried out in protest because the man had let go of her hand, but this dream made her inconsolable for quite some time. When I made inquiries, she could only give me one word at a time with moaning tears between each word: 'playing,' 'soldier,' 'leg,' and lastly, 'healing,'" Hannah's voice quivered with emotion as she remembered her daughter's pain-filled cries.

Yaron put his arm around his trembling wife for comfort. "I remembered the story quite well," he began when Hannah's body felt at peace. "As I was outside one hot day, Abia came out to the courtyard with your broomstick. It was tucked under her arm and she tried to dance with it. Finding it too difficult, she stopped dancing to walk with it instead," he concluded with a puzzled shake of his head.

"Then there was the one with the wicked woman dressed in gold who danced in a palace. And then there was another dream that seemed rather silly one about the same man in her dreams dancing with a dead tree," Hannah recalled, heavy-eyed.

"One of her dreams had the whole family in it," Yaron said with a yawn. "It seems we were in a room filled with other people and on the top of each head was a single glowing flame," he concluded with a sleepy smile. Reaching for his wife's warm hand, he ended the conversation. The night was too far spent to try to put together the puzzle pieces of Abia's dreams. Morning would come soon enough to begin another day, God willing. Maybe they would make sense of them then.

Introduction

Little did her parents know that Abia's dreams were a foretelling of events yet to come that involved the calling of a new type of worshiper, a prophetic dancer. This young Jewish girl's prophecy will have a profound impact on her life, but the message here is not for her alone. The prophetic messages in the series of dreams she experienced as a young child will be used to teach and to mature her in the faith.

This message explains the will of God for His people to worship Him, and portrays many facets of God's grace to His people. He has given us, His people, the awesome privilege to worship Him; but to dance with Him—that is truly sublime!

Much can be learned by studying the words and actions of God. When a message is sent from His own mouth to a prophet, who in turn becomes the spokesperson for God to His people, it is very revealing. One is given an opportunity to glimpse into the very heart of His heart. The emotions of God can be seen through the passionate way in which He speaks to His children. His desires are exposed. His intense love, joy, hatred, compassion, and anger all reveal parts of His unfathomable heart of love. Even our gift of free will shows how He wants love to be gifted back to Him.

The prophet Joel proclaimed a day of the Lord that was to come where the Spirit of God would be poured out on all humankind. Sons and daughters would prophecy, old men would dream dreams, and young men would see visions. Even on the male and female servants, God's Spirit would be poured out, and those who called on the name of the Lord would be delivered. Just as with all prophetic words, Joel gave the word without knowing when it would come to pass. Some words are fulfilled quickly while others take time, having to wait for the exact moment in the history deemed right by God.

The prophet Jeremiah testified of a time yet to be as well. Israel's mourning would one day be turned to joy with God's promises resounding throughout the generations and God's everlasting love for His people realized. He saw a future time when the people of God would be drawn by His loving kindness. Jeremiah understood the longing in the heart of God to one day take His beloved Israel's hand and dance with her on her rebuilt streets.

For many people, prophecies are figurative, reflecting deep hidden meanings that can only be obtained by the truly spiritual. Prophecies are figurative at times, but they can also be literal. God wants to dance with His people!

As Abia's life unfolds, her prophetic gift and calling to dance has to find its way through a maze of life's circumstances that seem to be at odds with the ways of God. A prophecy, like a child, matures to its fullest destiny and purpose when the baby is wanted, valued, carried to full term, delivered, fed, nurtured, instructed, guided, and taught in the ways of God. That is why satan loves abortion: it kills the potential for God's destiny and purpose before they are ever allowed to be birthed. But he is no match for our God. His people will dance on Jerusalem's restored streets and undoubtedly at the Marriage Supper of the Lamb.

A prophetic word from God has a life span that can cross generations because His word does not come back void, and it is powerful to press on until its purpose is accomplished. One generation can pay little attention to the word, causing it to become dormant for a generation or many generations. This will continue forward until such a time when God chooses someone else to carry on where the last person failed. When a person is in such agreement with the word, they are willing to persevere, despite all odds, to see the word to its completion.

Some people seem to have an easy time of finding their talent, gifting, purpose, or destiny in the Body of Christ. They find their voices to preach, sing, or teach. Some find an outreach ministry that it a perfect fit. Administration or helps may be their sweet spot and are used mightily. Others know immediately the instrument they will play to worship the Lord. How about you? Is your destiny still unfulfilled? The writer of Psalm 149:3 says, *"Let them praise His name with dancing…."* Some would say this is a suggestion, while others would say it is a command.

Could it be that you have not yet found your instrument because your instrument is your body and it is to be used to dance before the Lord? Ecclesiastes 3:4 says there is *"a time to dance."* Isn't it time you danced?

Abia has been chosen. She is to dance with and for the Lord. Take away the historical setting and Abia's story might be yours. You may have a season of mourning over body issues, sin's destruction, lost potential, or missed opportunities to fulfill what God has called you to, but Jesus is patiently waiting. He will make a way when there seems to be no way in sight. Turning is a dance move. He turns our mourning into dancing. We can be reassured that if we are *Dancing with Jesus,* we never dance alone.

CHAPTER I

Herod Antipas' Palace and Akil

"I must be dreaming!" Abia exclaimed as she and her siblings stood on the first step of the massive steps that led to King Herod's spectacular palace.

Twenty-five-year-old Samuel rolled his eyes at his younger sister's comment and said in big brother fashion, "It has been 12 years since you had a series of dreams, Abia. You are no longer 5, but 17, and you must hurry up!" he said to Abia with a scowl they both knew meant nothing.

"If you are dreaming, I am dreaming too!" chimed in Judith, the youngest at 15, as she peered at the beauty set before her.

"We must find Akil, and please remember everything Papa said to us before we left home," Samuel begged his two sisters as the weight of the responsibility of being the oldest began to fall on his shoulders.

Akil was the head man for all planned social events for King Herod and his queen. This was the man their Papa had warned them about. Suddenly the information their Papa had given about this man came rushing to Abia's remembrance. They were not to displease this man in any manner and were to leave the specially commissioned hand-sewn items they had worked on so diligently to Akil's capable care.

Abia's mind whirled with tidbits of information she had gathered about the palace, the delivery plans, and the man named Akil as they spent hours sewing and discussing and planning today's event. The collection of information her Papa had received came from friends in the marketplace where he sold his wares, from clients who loved to have something to pass on to those who would listen, and from palace slaves and servants who frequented the marketplace with daily updates from the palace.

In the presence of the palace, Abia recalled the fascinating story. As the palace supervisor and head of all functions regarding the royal family of Herod and his wife, Herodias, Akil had become quite used to being obeyed. He had earned superior rank and was highly trained from having been born in the house of Herod. He was supplied with whatever was necessary to make any occasion grand, but this one was extremely important, and he used whatever skills were necessary to get the job done, even if it involved fear or intimidation.

Akil and Queen Herodias, as she preferred to be called, had been planning the governor's birthday festivities for months. Never in the many years of his service to the royal family had so much effort been made for a birthday. The heavy burden to have everything completed to perfection was directly transferred from the queen onto Akil's proficient shoulders. He had steadily earned her trust from the first days she moved into the palace after becoming Herod Antipas' new wife. Although he had earned authority, Akil was still a slave in the house of Herod. Herodias held great power and could easily have him killed without fore-thought. He was not given the freedom or privilege to appeal to her with reason and logic, but was forced to comply with her every whim. Life went well in the palace when Queen Herodias was satisfied; this he and the other slaves and servants comprehended very well.

Akil had vast experience with Roman nobility and knew their expensive tastes, which made him valuable, but not invaluable. As long as he did his job well, he lived. As long as the slaves given to his charge did their jobs well, they lived. However, the great strain and heavy responsibility to meet the ever-increasing demands grew by the hour.

The queen seemed obsessed with having everything done to perfection. Just when Akil considered the arrangements entirely complete, believing the queen could not get any more specific and detailed, a new set of instructions would come, as if the same time allotment applied.

No one knew what compelled her to change her mind so frequently. Such was the case of her latest changes in the royal table linens. From red trimmed with gold to blue and white, the queen left the royal seamstresses with immediate order changes, causing great turmoil among the women. The complaint from the head seamstress was valid: there was not enough time to try to duplicate the color blue the queen had in mind and have the linens sewn in time for the celebration.

Abia remembered her Momma giving her own valuable pieces of information that she had gleaned daily from her friends and the women at the marketplace. She proudly filled in parts of the story Papa was too humble to tell. She was proud of Papa and the family who meant everything to her.

The story continued with Akil's dilemma about the new orders given by Queen Herodias to change the color scheme of the dinner linens. It was reported to Momma that Akil suddenly remembered a local man whose workmanship he had greatly admired and whose location was convenient, which could help with the issue of time. Yaron Ben-David and his family were one of the few able to reproduce the specific color of blue the queen was insistent upon. In order to appease Herodias and get the job done in a timely fashion, Akil authorized assigning the task to a local Hebrew family.

Yaron Ben-David and his family's reputation was renowned for their creation of incredible handmade fine fabrics with expertise in methods to dye the materials to suit the taste of the richest families of Galilee and surrounding regions. Yaron's eye for detail and impeccable taste seemed to match Akil's own, and his admiration of the man and his family had grown with each item of craftsmanship he had seen through the years. Their talents included creative design and dress making, fabrication of sturdy cushion upholstery, impressive sails for fishermen's boats and royal ships alike, and lovely personalized embroidery. Their needlecrafts were well known as pieces of art. Herod Antipas owned a red robe of their making—one of better-quality than any he had ever seen.

It was said of the Yaron Ben-David family that they seemed to possess an almost divine aptitude for anything they put their hands to do. Yaron Ben-David, when complimented on his craft, gave honor and credit to his God. Rumor had it that Yaron Ben-David and his family attributed all success to God, their one and only God, from whom they believed all talents and blessing flowed. Akil, a slave born in the house of Herod from Egyptian parents, knew little of such matters. The other marketplace servants and slaves did not understand it either, nor did they seem to care about the Hebrews' religion or their God. Divinely inspired or not, it was agreed by all who saw the handiwork of the Ben-David family that their work was always impeccable.

As Abia gathered her thoughts to the present, she also tried to gather the linens she was holding to keep them from dropping to the ground. The items were indeed beautiful. She glanced down for the last time at the fabrics her family had handled for weeks. It was always bittersweet and emotional for her when it was time for the fabrics to be delivered. Each sewing project was an act of worship for her and her family. She knew the new owners of these wonderful pieces would not have the same appreciation for them. Indeed, some of the people attending this party would be quite upset if they knew Jewish hands had touched the items. This party was for King Herod's glory, not God's.

Herod's royal emblem was painstakingly embroidered on each table covering. The wide, stuffed dining cushions for the floor were upholstered in blue and white and would provide each royal guest comfort while eating and during after-dinner entertainment. The towels were guaranteed to dry the hands of the most prominent of guests without complaint. The soft, white linen napkins would provide each woman with a beautiful memento of the evening and double as container to hold all of the special party trinkets the rich had come to expect from generous hosts. King Herod would receive all the recognition and honor for his generosity in providing his guests with such beauty.

As the three Ben-David offspring held in their arms evidence of their workmanship soon to be handed over to Akil, they each exchanged knowing glances. Whenever a project was completed, it was their custom to offer a quick prayer to God for the ability and strength. As they lifted their eyes Heavenward in a silent prayer, it was as if to also say, "May all glory and honor be God's."

Knowing the celebration would begin shortly and their wares were urgently needed, Samuel, Abia, and Judith finished their climb up the palace steps and hurried toward their planned meeting with Akil.

CHAPTER 2

Yaron Ben-David's Royal Commission

Akil's visit two weeks prior to the royal banquet came as quite a surprise to the Ben-David family. When the royal commission had come personally by Akil, head social planner for the royal family, life was suddenly turned upside down. Yaron dismissed all but Samuel from the room when the booming knock from the door sounded his arrival. Samuel was allowed to stay in the room with Yaron as Akil handpicked the exact fabric and color for each item given to him by Queen Herodias for Herod's birthday celebration. Yaron seemed as impressed with Akil's keen eye and high-quality taste as Akil was with the Ben-David's home stitchery business.

All business agreements and all transactions were made by Yaron. It was unusual for Yaron to take such a demanding job, especially with such impossible time restrictions. His demand for perfection and insistence upon quality would make this order especially difficult. Yet, this order was not so much a request, but a demand from the royal palace, as conveyed by Akil coming to place the order himself. One could not afford to make enemies with the royal household, Yaron reasoned. There was enough strife in the region as it was. He assured Akil the job would be done in the allotted time and that the quality of the work would not suffer. He also said the items would be hand-delivered to the palace kitchen and into Akil's hands directly.

As Hannah, Judith, and Abia listened to the muffled voices from the adjoining bedroom, through a yellow muslin curtain, they began to pray. Fulfilling the confident promises Yaron made to Akil would require God's guidance, strength, and assistance.

As Akil left their house the females of the family strained to catch a glimpse of him. All they could make out was that the man was black, very tall, and wearing a colorful orange turban wrapped around a black head. Two men, who were traveling with him, quickly turned their attention to him as he approached. Bowing low, they followed Akil as he briskly made his way back toward the palace gate.

Yaron and Samuel quickly gathered the three into the kitchen room, knowing well how curious they would be to hear what business transaction had been made with the house of Herod. As was his custom, Yaron mentally assessed the materials needed for the task and the family member who possessed special aptitude for each assignment. Time was short, but the quality could not be compromised.

Yaron looked to his wife with mixed excitement and concern gleaming from his eyes. "I want you, Hannah, to immediately start on designing a template of the royal crest to these specifications," he said as he handed Hannah a piece of parchment containing a drawing of the intricate and complicated crest. She took it from his hand and tenderly touched his cheek, conveying a silent message of understanding and acceptance.

Yaron turned his gaze toward Abia to give the sewing assignment he had for her, but before he could speak, he beat his chest, and with his voice filled with emotion, he said, "Abia, my Abia!" with small tears blurring his vision. As his watery eyes scanned his daughter's form, tears of gratitude began to fall in earnest as he raised his hands in worship to God. "I praise my God for you, and I praise Him for the many blessings He has bestowed on this family throughout the years. But, when I see you standing without crutches, fully able to walk, my heart..." He brought his fist to rest on his heart and with his voice too full of emotion to finish his sentence, his eyes spoke of his heartfelt love for his daughter and his God.

It was wonderful for Abia to see tears of joy streaming down his face instead of the tears of sorrow he had shed for the past 12 years. After the accident that left Abia lame, the Ben-David family had grown quite accustomed to reading the expressions in people's eyes when they looked at Abia wherever she went. The looks hurt them all, but especially Abia.

Abia had witnessed the pitying looks in her family's eyes ever since the day of the accident, when she was five years old, and it was soon realized she would not be able to walk very well due to the hip injury. Worse still was the news that she would be unable to bear children when marrying age came.

As a man in a man's world, Yaron knew what that would mean for her. No young man would want to marry a young girl who could not give him sons, which every Hebrew man desired. "My poor, beautiful daughter," Yaron would say again and again as he shook his head from side to side with regret. Believing her fate was sealed that tragic day to become a spinster doomed to live out the rest of her life with her parents instead of having a family of her own brought great sadness to his heart. Yaron's emotions always shined brightly in his eyes. Until now, they always showed a mixture of sorrow and compassion for his daughter. He had felt sorry for her because he wanted for her what most fathers desire for their daughters at the age of 17; he wanted her married.

Jewish parents believed their daughters should be pledged to be married or already married at an early age. Hopefully they would have one or two children by the age of 17, which Abia now was. Yaron and Hannah considered motherhood to be one of the greatest honors God bestowed on women, especially if they produced sons. They did not want their daughter to miss out on receiving the love of a husband, becoming a wife, and motherhood.

Yaron and Hannah saw the emotional pain in Abia's eyes grow as the consequences of the accident became more fully understood over time. Despite her brave front and happy appearance, they knew her pain and watched helplessly.

"Amitz, Abia! Be brave, Abia," they would say to her in Hebrew when young girls would point at her or young boys would look at her with repulsion because of her limp. Even in her early teen years, they whispered the phrase of encouragement to her each time older women in the marketplace passed her by with eyes full of reproach, as if she were to blame for her troubles.

To avoid pain, both physically and emotionally, most days Abia stayed inside their home. Abia learned early on how to sew. It was something she could do easily without causing pain in her hip. Her parents taught her all they knew about sewing, weaving, designing, pressing flax seed into soft material, and many other elements of the highly skilled art of sewing and fabric-making.

Learning the trade came without difficulty. Abia's mind was sharp and seemed to grow with each new challenge. As the business grew, her parents depended more and more on her talents and skills. It was a relief to Hannah when Abia could assume some of her responsibilities of helping Yaron and Samuel with the sewing, which allowed Hannah more time to manage home duties.

Although it was difficult to admit, it also afforded her more time to teach Judith the skills she would one day need when she would become some young man's wife. It saddened Hannah's heart to think that her beautiful Abia would never need the skills she could teach her. Hannah was practical enough to know that, although it left her older daughter out, she had to teach the skills to Judith, who was already pledged to be married to Abraham, the baker's son. They would be married soon after her 16th birthday.

As Abia scanned the kitchen room and met the faces of the people she loved best in the world, her heart filled with joy once more. Her life had been full and happy despite the unfortunate circumstances that left her lame for so many years. *How wonderful to have a family to share love and pain with*, she thought to herself. Since she had regained the usage of her hips, she realized how truly blessed she had been. Abia had parents who loved her and never left her side. Her brother, Samuel, would move Heaven and Earth if it were within his power to do so for her. Her dear sister, Judith, loved her so much that she even hid her own excitement about her upcoming wedding out of fear that it would hurt Abia's feelings.

How wonderful to be able to truly celebrate Judith's pending marriage with a joyful heart instead of the fake smile Abia showed that fooled no one. And on the day when Judith and Abraham would make her an aunt, she could now literally jump for joy.

"I need you, Abia, to choose the correct thread strength and thickness," Yaron instructed loudly, bringing everyone back to the matters at hand as he swiftly wiped the last of his tears into his sleeve. "Make the colors vibrant and colorful. Center the crest and design a trim that will frame and enhance it. Make it unlike any other!" he said, fully confident in her abilities and smiling with joy that overflowed from his heart.

Abia's smile seemed to bring him a measure of reassurance and the support he needed. Yaron quickly shared with Abia and

Hannah the rest of the directions and details, including the number of table covers that would be needed, the precise position of the crest for each, and the table size.

"The royal crest will be sewn to our highest quality, brightest white linen table covers," Papa spoke to them all.

"Judith," his voice was still somber, but softened as his youngest child of 15 approached him for her individual instructions. It was a bittersweet time for him as he remembered this was probably the last time they would all be working together as family.

"I am placing you in charge of the napkins and towels," he said good-heartedly. "You will embroider an elaborate 'H' on the corner of each one." Judith nodded her agreement as small pools of tears began to form in her dark brown eyes. She realized this was to be her last sewing job with her family. It hurt her to know she would no longer be a part of the work her family did, and she would also miss the family comradery. Judith would no longer take her place among the Ben-David household, but would take her place with her beloved Abraham and his household. As the wife of the baker's son, she would learn new work in baking, which she was learning to love as she worked diligently beside Abraham and her new family.

Abraham's father, Adam Ben-Daniels, was joyful and funny, and Judith already adored him. His positive outlook on life brought just the right balance to his wife's colorful, but flighty personality. Mora loved people, but she was a gossip. She delighted in sharing any bit of information she had with the willing and unwilling alike. Mora had a kind heart, and when the time came, she would make a wonderful grandmother for Abraham and Judith's children. With a smile on her face, Judith thought that maybe having grandchildren to kiss would keep her lips too busy to indulge in chin wagging. If not, she knew Abraham would be more than willing to escape his mother's roof and come for frequent and more peaceful visits at her parents' home.

Samuel had been in the meeting with Akil and Yaron and knew the guidelines for the overly stuffed floor cushions that the patrons would sit upon while they ate. They were to be upholstered with heavy wool dyed blue and white pieces sewn together, creating a pattern of stripes. Finding the right color of dyes to match the customer's need was his specialty. This would be his assignment, and he looked forward to the challenge in front of him. He was eager to get the project started, especially knowing he would participate in the delivery of the wares to Herod's palace when they were completed. This rare treat was exciting, and he knew the opportunity to visit behind the king's palace was not afforded to many, especially Jews. He was proud of his family and the workmanship of their hands. Determined to do his very best, he was eager to get started with the monumental project.

Once the overall instructions were given to each member of the family, they bowed their heads as Yaron petitioned God for help and favor. For indeed, to accomplish such a feat, God's help was required.

For the next two weeks, no one paid but brief visits to their beds. When the sun rested from its long day, oil lamps were lit throughout the room, giving it a bright, friendly glow to continue the sewing. Throbbing fingers, aching backs, and near exhaustion plagued the whole family. The sun poured in through the windows and then darkened them when nighttime advanced, giving a continual report and reminder of the time that was quickly slipping away.

Allowing only short, periodic breaks to grab a quick bite to eat or stretch sore bodies from the strain of sitting in one position for long periods of time, they pressed on. Just when fatigue would begin to crash down upon them like violent waves hitting the rocky shore, Yaron and Samuel would start to sing. Their deep, rich voices sang songs of gratitude for the work, for the ability and talents to accomplish the work, and most of all, thanksgiving to their God and Creator of all. Worshiping God was as natural and normal a part of their daily lives as their need to eat or sleep. Soon, the women would join their voices to the male ones, and together they would harmonize flawlessly from the many years of practice while working alongside each other.

Singing certainly helped break the monotony of sewing one stitch followed by another. It also helped them to remember that, while they were hired by a man for the job they could do, ultimately they were doing the job as if they were doing it for God Himself. Using meticulous skill and care, they pressed onward to complete the task. They were determined to accomplish the ambitious assignment and to complete it in the allotted time promised to Akil. The Ben-Davids worked as a team; they worked as a family.

As a family, they did everything together because their work allowed them the opportunity. They ate, played, laughed, cried, and sewed together. At times it did not seem like work at all. It was how they spent their lives, and it was all they had ever known.

Hannah and Yaron were wonderful storytellers, and often time was spent telling and listening to Jewish history and oral accounts passed from one generation to the next. The Torah was taught in such a manner, and everyone loved listening as the stories and characters came alive with their words pictures

After the Torah, Abia's and Judith's next favorite stories were when their parents shared with the family tales of times long ago. Stories of young Yaron and Hannah when first married were the most endearing to the two. Hannah usually told the stories aloud while Yaron shook his head in embarrassment of his impetuous, youthful antics. On occasion, Yaron would chime in with a correction to Hannah's story when he believed she was exaggerating or when he thought she was telling too many private details of the story.

One day Hannah began to recount a story from when she and Yaron were quite young and first married. Yaron and Hannah had learned the art of sewing through necessity, Hannah recalled. A series of setbacks when they were first married caused Yaron to change occupations. Her husband had been a fisherman, like his father before him, who fished the unpredictable seas off the coast of Galilee. A sudden, raging storm fueled by the heated winds of eastern Egypt overturned Yaron's boat one dark day, leaving him to swim to shore. Nothing was saved but his life.

As hard as he tried, Yaron seemed unable to find work fishing. Some of the superstitious fishermen thought Yaron was a carrier of bad luck. They reasoned that because he had the misfortune of sinking his own boat, they would not allow him to work with them in theirs. Some fishermen with large families simply had no room for any additional helpers.

Yaron could barely keep food in their stomachs, and when Samuel was born, it became more and more difficult. He did odd jobs as often as he could, but they were few and far between. Hannah took in sewing jobs from other women, often in exchange for food. She grew in reputation as a fine seamstress. Yaron was not at all happy with this because he believed the man should be the one to support his family, not the wife. He often expressed his displeasure to Hannah, especially when the other men in the village made fun of him. "*Yarn* Ben-David," they would say, making sport of his first name, Yaron. He was humiliated and became desperate.

Since Yaron had no money and had no way to purchase another boat, he finally decided it was time to pray for help. As he sat on a rock at the water's edge praying, out of the corner of his eye he saw a sudden flash of something shiny. The sun's reflection bounced from something very small just a short distance from where he sat. He instinctively crossed the distance in search of the tiny object on the beach, his prayers completely forgotten.

Feeling discouraged and with little else to do to occupy his time, he began to search for the article in the hot sand. After about 15 minutes, he was ready to give up; he had convinced himself that he was a failure. If he could not retrieve something as big as his boat from the bottom of the sea; how did he think he could find something little on a beach covered with sand? In defeat, he fell back into the hard sand. Extending both hands slightly behind him to break his fall, he sat down, and as he did, his right hand immediately began to hurt.

Looking at his hand in disgust, he saw the small object he had been looking for painfully imbedded in his palm. His self-pity suddenly interrupted, he paused to investigate. Buried into his leathery hand, calloused from years of hard work, was a needle. It was a sewing needle like the one used to mend tattered fishing nets and repair sails for small boats.

"Wonderful," he said sarcastically, "my wife's sewing has been a pain to my pride, and now a sewing needle is a pain in my hand!"

Suddenly, he jumped to his feet and spun round and round with his hands extended in praise as his mind began to clear.

As his knees met the beach that day, he remembered part of a story from the Torah. Long ago the prophet Moses was being instructed by God before he faced the pharaoh. Moses was not confident in himself or what to do next. Moses had been given a new rod or staff of authority by God. The Lord spoke a reminder to Moses saying, "What is that in thine hand?"

"Yaron Ben-David!" he shouted to himself, "What is that in thine hand?" Suddenly he knew what he was to do with his life. He would take the needle from his hand, swallow his pride, and do the very thing every fisherman all around the world already knew how to do: he would sew.

Little by little, his skills grew with each new job he acquired. He learned he was very skilled at the art of sewing, and his work became known throughout the village. At first he sewed only those things having to do with the fishing trade, but gradually he and Hannah joined forces and developed their skills together. They slowly expanded their sewing business to include awning-making, covering stuffed cushions with upholstery, sails for large ships, creating new fabrics, inventing new dyes and dyeing techniques, making prayer shawls, spinning, and also designing the latest fashions for rich men and women alike. Window screens, which allowed breezes in and kept insects out, were a specialty.

A modest living was made, but as the business expanded, it became apparent the extra pairs of hands of their children were needed. So as soon as possible they taught each of their children different skills that matched their individual strengths and aptitudes. They each agreed that working together as a family was a blessing for them all.

That night, as they were seated together with a small fire lit for warmth from the sudden coolness of the air, they did as they had always done. They sewed; only this time they were sewing for the governor of Galilee's birthday party. The Ben-David wares would be on display for all of the richest people in the region to see. The business that might be generated from having such a rich client who others wanted to emulate might cause their business to prosper like never before. God was in charge of the family business, and if it grew, it was because of His help. And to think, this would never have been possible if Yaron had not looked at what was in his hand!

CHAPTER 3

Sunrise, Bring Us Peace

It was a great tribute in many respects to be given the royal commission for their sewing wares by Akil, from the palace of Herod, but it was with mixed feelings that Yaron accepted the work. Whatever monetary favor was received from the work would be welcomed and much needed, but it was not certain any money would be paid at all. As he sewed, Yaron considered many possibilities, but each with the same negative conclusion

The taxes could be removed prior to payment; therefore, very little or no money at all would find its way to Yaron's pocket. It was also within the realm of possibility that the royal palace might consider their hard work and craftsmanship to be a contribution to the governor's birthday celebration. The palace might reason that, having been granted the distinct honor and privilege, the Ben-David family would be insulted by an offer of payment; consequently, none would be given. Yaron's opinions turned from sarcastic to fearful as he considered the outcome if he dared to refuse. To offend any of the Herod family could prove fatal for him or any member of the Ben-David family.

As unreasonable as the dealings were, little could be done to rectify the mistreatment. "Such is the way it is for Jews everywhere," Yaron reasoned. Trouble was beginning to brew on every cobblestone street of Jerusalem.

Yet, the unwarranted abusive treatment of the Jewish people by the Herod family was not unique in their lifetime. Herod Antipas, a crafty, devious, self-satisfying ruler, was in many ways no match for his father, Herod Antipater, or as he had preferred to be called, Herod the Great.

The Roman Empire had taken over the country of Judea many years ago. Marc Anthony in Rome appointed Herod Antipater as king of the Jews. Although he was not fully Jewish, he made many attempts to give the illusion of being Jewish. Seeing himself as both the Jews' political ruler and their spiritual ruler as well, King Herod believed he could be worshiped as their Jewish god. This required unquestioning respect and devotion necessary from his Jewish subjects, no matter the cost.

King Herod set out to gain the Jews' favor. He restored and rebuilt the great Temple in Jerusalem to its former splendor as under Solomon. He employed thousands of Jewish men as masons, carpenters, and other skilled laborers for his ambitious building project. He developed an intricate city water system for Jerusalem and owned a monopoly over the asphalt removed from the Dead Sea for use in shipbuilding projects which employed many others.

Antipater's ambition to build, however, was not for pleasing the Jews. He needed the Jews for their strong backs and refined skills to promote himself among the most elite. He frantically set out to satisfy his own quest for fame, but by doing so, he desired to impress Rome with the unprecedented growth and construction of cities, palaces, fortresses, and countless other huge building projects. This brought King Herod tremendous political and governmental influence and power, and his kingdom grew in unparalleled ways. This growth required enormous manpower with unrestrained and continuous financial provision, which was extorted from the Jewish people. A heavy tax burden was made mandatory by King Herod and collected by Roman soldiers. The profits from the trade and extensive taxes made Herod and Rome wealthy, resulting in more outlandish edifices, roadways, and countless construction efforts. The kingdom was increasing in riches, and King Herod was an ever-increasing, high-ranking ruler.

Manipulation and greed were powerful tools in the hands of King Herod. He allowed nothing or no one to get in his way. Extreme suspicion and jealousy of all alleged friends, family, and foes caused the king to execute cruel methods to maintain control and power over his kingdom. Herod Antipater became obsessively more anxious, and his distrust of other people, their thoughts, and their motives increased to the point of mental illness and madness. Plagued with severe itching, feet tumors, ulcers, sexual madness, chronic kidney disease with gangrene, and worms, his mental condition was twisted and tortured.

After killing his wife's brother and his own two sons, Herod became infuriated when his wife and her mother's cries of grief could be heard throughout the palace halls. When his wife finally stopped sharing his bed, his jealous rage became violent and unstoppable. He soon had her and her mother executed. Afterward, he was known to wildly run about his bedroom, believing they were haunting him in the night with strategies of murder. His enemies increased in number.

Despite his attempts to deceive the Jews, his schemes were quickly exposed. Resentment and hatred for the king was widespread, and his blatant disregard for Jewish customs, traditions, and laws was made evident each day. Social unrest was rampant. When King Herod put a huge Roman eagle at the main entrance of the Temple in Jerusalem at Pentecost and required the Jewish people to worship it, they rebelled with rioting in the streets. Upon getting the news, Rome sent troops to brutally put down the revolt, and over 2,000 Jews were murdered by sword or crucifixion.

Despite the cruel methods he exercised over the Jewish people, Herod's fears continued to increase. He saw everyone as a threat to him or to his kingdom. Many fathers, mothers, grandparents, and siblings continued to grieve for the children who had been slain by the hands of King Herod when he sought to kill the baby boy who was said to be King of the Jews in Jerusalem.

Herod had ten wives over time who provided him with many children. Many of them were executed or exiled from his kingdom. His first son, Antipater, his namesake, and his mother were banished when the child was quite young. When Herod was old and sickness had taken its revenge on this wicked and cruel king, he called his son back to his side in order to bequeath to him the entire kingdom. But Herod uncovered a plot by Antipater to kill his own father, so he executed Antipater and named Herod Antipas his successor. A few days later, the elder Herod died.

However, altogether King Herod had made five different wills, so the decision to divide the kingdom fell to the Roman Emperor Augustus. Not trusting the sons of Herod, fearing them to be like their father, Augustus finally honored Herod's last will. He named the three sons as tetrarchs, or governors, rather than kings, and divided the land among them.

Herod Antipas became Galilee's tetrarch and tried to avoid offending his Jewish subjects for a long while. Although not cruel or violent like his father before him, Antipas harbored hopes of being made king. Therefore, he wanted his part of the kingdom to grow and for Rome to be impressed with his management of the region.

"It is difficult to understand the foreign occupation in our land when our fathers were promised this land by God centuries ago. Such is the way of our people," Yaron explained the next evening while they were sewing.

His story continued as the family listened. Jews had been persecuted by others in their own land repeatedly; now it seemed to be Rome's turn.

Many of the Jewish people and leaders were growing angrier with the constant disregard of the Jewish people, their Law, and their customs. Antipas' own father had done many atrocities to the Jewish people for generations, causing distrust and hatred. And just like his father, Antipas' suspicions were on the rise.

Herod Antipas seemed to fear some Jewish men whose growing popularity caused him great concern over possible uprising and civil disobedience. Rome thought it tedious to continue assisting Antipas with potential trouble stemming from the Jews, and they sent Roman soldiers to police the area to prevent all disorderly conduct.

To keep the Jewish people from growing in power and influence, the soldiers manned positions all over the region. Their presence was seen in the marketplace, along fishing villages, in small townships, and near the local synagogues. One could not step into Jerusalem without sensing the growing tension.

"The Roman army has caused much suffering among our people," Yaron said. The family enjoyed learning about their history, so he continued his narrative as they sewed on into the wee hours of the morning.

It did not take long for the whole region of Galilee to be in constant fear of the Roman soldiers. The soldiers were regularly looking for the slightest movements among the Jews indicating anti-Roman sentiment, and they used cruel methods to silence them.

More alarming and hurtful than the Roman home rule was how fellow Jews were pitted against one another. This caused the soldiers to get involved in Jewish internal disagreements and to intervene when quarrels got out of hand.

One man who was growing in recognition and fame was a man named John. From the barren region of the rugged hills and valleys of Judea, John was thought of by many Jews to be very much like the prophet Elijah, who prophesied of a forerunner to announce the long-awaited Messiah. John the Baptist, as people were calling him, had an ability to disturb people—faithful Jews and fallen Jews alike.

The two most prominent religious groups in Israel that John spoke out against were the Pharisees and Sadducees. The Pharisees, whom John criticized for being legalistic and hypocritical, followed the letter of the Law, but ignored its true intent. John criticized the Sadducees for using religion to promote their political position. He made enemies from both sides. When John proclaimed a local man named Jesus as the Messiah, people from all viewpoints became riled.

As Yaron's story concluded, everyone became lost in their own thoughts, for he had given them much to think about. Within the safety of the kitchen room it was difficult to fathom the depths of unrest that lay so close to their own door. Peace was never anything one should take for granted.

The family had seen the Roman guards quite often in the last few months parading in public to prevent heated religious debates from resulting in scuffles. The turbulent times in which they lived made peace a valuable commodity.

Peace. That word had not been one the Ben-David family or the Jewish people had really ever known, but it was constantly sought. Their family was devout and they trusted in the God of Abraham, Isaac, and Jacob. They believed God's promises given throughout the centuries. Day and night they were taught of a special day to come when God would send a righteous King to reunite God with His people, and in that day, peace would again come. This anointed King, they were taught, would lead the Jews and would establish justice in the world. The Messiah would liberate their country, its people, and the world, and He would bring blessed peace.

The synagogues were exploding with a renewed interest in ancient prophets and their prophecies. While many people were unsettled, every Jew could agree on one thing. As night fell each evening, there was a renewed hope and desperation for the following sunrise to be the promised day of peace and the coming Messiah.

CHAPTER 4

John,
the Wilderness Crier

As with most busy families, the events of the day are not always shared with other members of the family in detail as much as one would desire. Time simply does not permit it. Daily chores and routines consume the day, and before they knew it, one day would slide into another and weeks would go by—leaving them to scratch their heads and wonder where the time went.

In the months prior to the royal commissioning for Herod's birthday celebration, much was happening in Galilee. It was not until the Ben-David family gathered together to do the sewing for the event that they had the opportunity to talk about the significant events that were happening almost daily around them. Sewing for Herod's party afforded the Ben-David family time to get caught up on the events of the past few months.

Sample pieces of fabric were soaking in dye kettles containing different ingredients, in the attempt to produce just the right combination of colors needed for Akil's order. Many different ingredients—flower heads, roots, wood ash, lime, henna, berries, bark from trees, and many others in combination—could produce different shades of a variety of colors. The right color was being sought, and it was necessary to create a set of color batches in order to make the right choice. Samuel and Yaron continuously stirred the pots with wooden paddles.

As Yaron stirred, he had eager listeners to any story he wanted to tell. So much was happening around them; the stories were hardly ever ones they heard more than once, but they did not seem to mind hearing some stories over and over again. Such was the case with the next story.

Yaron, a few months earlier, had come home from the market street to tell Hannah of news he had heard on the streets, as was his daily routine. He had made plans to gather with many men by the waters of the Jordan River to listen to the bizarre man who spoke straight to the hearts of Jewish people. The whole city was buzzing with tales of the peculiar man known by the name John.

"He was a rather strange man, the man named John," Yaron remarked quite candidly to his wife. As he related the facts and the opinions he had heard from the men in the marketplace, Hannah also shared the stories she'd heard from the women who sold wares in the shops where she did her daily shopping. Together they retold for Samuel, Judith, and Abia the rather incredible story of the stranger named John.

It was said that John had lived in the barren wilderness area of Judea and was sustained by eating honey and locusts. Clothed in a tunic made of camel hair tied with a leather belt, he was different from any priest the people had ever known. His preaching was powerful, and when multitudes of people gathered to hear him, they formed varied opinions of him. Not all judgments being formed were based merely on what he wore.

Many thought he was the incarnate prophet Elijah who had been taken up by God and was never buried. Some agreed that he was the prophet Elijah, but for a different reason. They believed he was Elijah because he stood up against evil rulers when he preached. Many others thought he was the man prophesied by the prophet Isaiah seven centuries before as the forerunner of the Messiah. Others believed him to be the messenger prophesied by Malachi whom God would send to clear the way for the Messiah. When some said he was the son of Zachariah, the elderly priest, others thought it ridiculous because no one that strange could be anyone other than a foreigner.

Yaron seemed to agree that John was the son of the elderly priest Zachariah and his wife, Elizabeth. He and Hannah had told many stories throughout the years to their children about the remarkably faithful couple and their miraculous son.

Zachariah had been the high priest of the Jewish people some 30 years earlier. Yaron first remembered hearing about him when Zachariah was an old priest who served God faithfully in the Temple for many years. He and his wife, Elizabeth, were not able to have children. Despite the advice of others, Zachariah did not divorce Elizabeth; they stayed true to the belief that God would one day hear their prayers and give them a son.

When Zachariah entered the Temple to perform his priestly duty to burn incense, Gabriel, an angel of the Lord, appeared to Zachariah. He told him that the Lord had heard their petition. They would be granted a son, and he was to name his son John. The Lord said John would be great in the sight of the Lord, that he was not to drink wine or liquor, and that he would be filled with the Holy Spirit while yet in his mother's womb. John would be used by God to turn the hearts of many sons and daughters of Israel back to the Lord their God. He would have the style and strength of the prophet Elijah. He would preach about how the old sinful life would be washed away after people repented of their sins. Repentance for the remission of sins and baptism to wash away the old sinful life were to be his life's message and mission.

Zachariah wondered about how this miracle baby was to be conceived because the couple was so old, so the angel of the Lord caused him not to speak until the baby was born. Zechariah then followed God's instructions to name the baby John instead of naming him after himself or giving him another family name. Zachariah's inability to speak caused everyone to believe that the old priest had indeed seen an angel of the Lord and had been told to call his son John.

When Zachariah finally began to talk again, his first words were praises to God. Having been filled by the Holy Spirit, he began to prophesy the coming of a Savior who would redeem His people. He foretold how his son, John, would prepare the way for the Messiah.

Yaron did not know much more of Zachariah's story until his own life was touched by the same cruel hand of fate two years after John's birth. A child born six months after John was known as the true King of the Jews. King Herod, who believed he was king of the Jews, was very threatened by this child. He ordered his soldiers to search the countryside for the two-year-old boy who had been born with the title he considered his. Herod did not want to meet the child; he wanted the child murdered. When the soldiers could not find the child, he ordered all children under the age of five to be massacred. Zachariah, like all fathers at the time, was afraid for his son John's life.

Yaron was 17 years old when Jonah, his youngest brother, and many more male children were killed as a result of Herod's wickedness.

"Sadness has been a heavy covering of grief worn by everyone who mourned the loss of a child, grandchild, or little brother since that horrible day," Yaron's voice shook with his shoulders as sorrow overtook him once again. Momma stood up from her chair to lay her head upon her husband's bowed one. Her eyes were red from tears that attempted, time and time again, to wash away the heartbreak experienced by the loss of her own playmates and cousins who were killed that day.

"Children," Momma's voice barely above a whisper continued, "your own Papa was an eyewitness to the slaughter. He was covered with his brother's blood. The soldiers forced your Papa to place in your father's arms the dead body of his little brother as punishment for trying to protect his own child and for not revealing the whereabouts of the new Jewish Messiah." Yaron's children gathered around their father and wept bitter tears.

"My children and dear wife," Yaron began slowly when his tears were spent. "I have such love and appreciation for my family who is drawn around me now. You bring such abundant joy to this man's broken heart. We live in desperate and evil times, yet we cannot forget the pain of God our Father who has been separated from His children by sin as my own father has known. God has promised the Messiah would come and save His people. It has been spoken by prophets of long ago that Jehovah would send a messenger one day who would point the way to the coming Messiah. For many years Jews have been faithfully watching and waiting. Many have gone to their graves and yet He has not come.

"In my lifetime I have seen death, yes. Yet, I am also seeing signs of life, new life," he remarked with new vigor in his voice. "An unexpected sound coming from a desert man is kindling a flame of hope in the hearts of many along Jordan's shores. The one they call John is awakening God's people like none I have seen in my years on this earth. Could it be God the Father can no longer stand the separation from His children and at long last has sent the messenger we have longed for?" As Yaron finished this part of the story, everyone's belief in God's faithfulness and love was once again renewed.

Yaron stopped stirring the fabric and pulled the dyed fabrics out from their dye kettles. He methodically hung them to dry outside the courtyard on clotheslines, making sure to remember from which kettle the individual sample cloths came in case the perfect color was achieved. He was glad for the break in the story because the retelling of the tragedy always left him feeling saddened for the brother he never knew.

With his emotions back in place, he entered the kitchen room to gather together more ingredient for the dyes. As he did, he continued telling the story. Yaron's story left off after telling about how John, as a young male child, was in danger like the others at the time. The young John had escaped the fate of so many others. But, Yaron remarked, the prophecy of Zachariah's son had not been fulfilled.

Now, at the age of 30, John's story continued as he began his ministry in the countryside after spending most of his life in the region's wilderness. People were curious about John and his message, including Yaron and Samuel, who later joined some of the men to hear for themselves what message was being proclaimed on Jordan's shores. The merely curious, the scholars, the religious, the skeptics, and the expectant came from far and near to hear more from this unusual man.

John's message was simple. He told the people—and by this he meant all the Jewish people—that they were living sinfully. God had tolerated it, but He would not be doing so much longer. A great and terrible day of judgment was to occur. Many believed him and wanted to know what they could do to be saved from the coming judgment day. Two things he said they could do. First, "Repent for the kingdom of God is at hand," John said, and second, "Be baptized."

The most highly religious among the Jewish people were shocked and took offense when he said that being descendants of Abraham was not good enough for God. John challenged them by saying that changes could not be made on the outside alone, but needed to be made from the inside. Confession of sin and a changed life always go together, he said.

The crowds questioned John about this. They wanted to know what they should do. John told the man who had two tunics that a changed life would cause him to share one with a man who had none. Likewise, a man who had food should do the same for one who was without. He advised some tax collectors who had come to be baptized to collect no more than what they had been ordered to collect. He told some soldiers not to take money from anyone by force or to accuse anyone falsely, but to be content with their wages.

The common people were astounded at his teachings. Numerous people proclaimed John to be the long-awaited Messiah, but he denied it. He only claimed to be a witness of the coming Christ and the one who would point the way to the Messiah when He came. John said his mission was to baptize with water, but the One coming would baptize by the Holy Spirit and with fire.

When John, the Baptizer, began to speak of reestablishing people's true relationship with God, some were overjoyed. The truly faithful were jubilant because the strain of trying to keep the Law was overwhelming and condemning.

Yaron shared with his wife about John's message. The two of them were among the first who went to be baptized by John in the Jordan River. They knew the sinful condition of their hearts, but they had not known a way to be clean, until now. At long last, humankind had a way back to God. God had made a way. The peace and love on their faces and the excitement from their testimonies were so obvious; their whole household went back to the Jordan River in the following days to learn and to be baptized.

As Yaron's story ended, it invoked much conversation among the family as each one remembered his or her own experience with being baptized by John at the river's edge. They each took turns reminiscing about the special occasion.

CHAPTER 5

A Lighter Load to Carry

The family laboriously continued to sew, design, and put together the pieces ordered by Akil for Herod's birthday celebration. The stories were a wonderful distraction from the hard work facing them, but more than that, they were stories that had changed their lives. Every remembrance of them brought back the experience as if it had just happened. It had been two months, but they felt they could tell these stories again and again and never grow tired of the telling.

The events of Abia's story occurred before she regained the use of her legs, but it was miraculous just the same. The message told by John had impacted her parents, but also the rest of their family. They too went to the banks of the Jordan and were also baptized. Abia's story picked up after her parents' baptism, but on the day when the rest of her family was baptized as well.

Abia was transported by a mule-drawn cart to the Jordan River. The cart was led by her brother, Samuel. Her parents and

Judith walked beside her as they traveled to the river bank. The distance was much too far for Abia to walk. Her injured hip and limp leg would have caused her great pain if she had tried.

At 17 years of age, she remained thankful for how wonderful her family had been to take care of her for the past 12 long years, especially Samuel. As the mule stirred the dirt with each step toward a new future, her memory was also stirred with past events.

The details of the accident were still very sketchy in Abia's mind. She remembered that she and Judith had been playing under a cart that Samuel had been loading to carry supplies to a nearby merchant. Samuel had warned the two young girls to come out of their hiding place, but as five- and three-year-olds are known to do from time to time, they ignored the wisdom of their older brother.

Just at that time, some type of commotion occurred. There was a horse, a soldier, and shouting. Judith ran out from under the cart ahead of Abia, but when Abia tried to follow her, the cart tipped over, trapping the frightened Abia beneath. She soon realized that she could not move any longer.

Abia heard laughing and more screams. As she looked up, she saw Samuel. His strong face had streams of tears running down from his pain-filled eyes. Her life had changed in a matter of moments, but so had his. Samuel was consumed with guilt when it was discovered that Abia would be unable to walk without the use of a crutch.

For 12 years Samuel had done everything he could to help Abia. He took wonderful care of her and tried to assist her while she was recovering. He was always there to retrieve things she could not reach. He often carried her on his back to go places and then helped her learn how to use a crutch when she was able. Abia thought he was the greatest brother alive. As time marched on, she learned that he had decided not to marry the baker's daughter,

Sarah, with whom he was so much in love, because of his sense of duty toward Abia.

Samuel had been 13 years old at the time of the accident and was now 25. Any childish and unfounded blame Abia had for Samuel when she was 5 was fleeting and had long since passed, but his guilt had not. Samuel the Dependable was once again true to his nickname. It hurt Abia to think of all the sacrifices he had made because of his love for her, but when she thought about him doing it out of a sense of responsibility because of his own guilt, it was too much to bear.

At long last, they arrived at the river. Many people were already there desiring to be baptized as well. When it was Samuel's turn to be baptized in the cool, fast-flowing water of the Jordan, it was Abia's heartfelt desire that all his guilt and pain would be washed away as well. Abia prayed that her brother could at last forgive himself.

On the river's edge, that bright, sunny day, Samuel found peace for the first time in 12 long, grueling years. As he looked up, with water dripping down his face, the sad tears had been replaced with tears of joy and acceptance. The dark heaviness of false guilt he had been carrying at long last drifted away with the currents. God's forgiveness permitted him to forgive himself.

When John had finished baptizing Samuel, he baptized Judith. She was drenched from head to toe, but as she came up from the cool water, with her hair dripping wet, she seemed more beautiful than ever.

Her beauty did not go unnoticed by her future husband, Abraham, who was watching from the water's banks. He was amazed at his good fortune to be betrothed to such a wonderful girl. He agreed she was indeed a beauty on the outside, but far surpassing the physical was the beauty she had from within. She would make a perfect mate for him. They shared a strong belief in God, and with the new teachings of John, Abraham looked forward to their life together.

As the water split around her, Judith began to worship God using the incredible gift He had given her. With her arms extended Heavenward, she opened her mouth to sing. Judith's voice was perfection and amazingly pure. Her deep love and gratefulness flowed within her, and she expressed it through song, just as King David had long ago.

The song she sang was from King David's own psalms, but the melody was her own:

The Lord is my shepherd,
I shall not want.
He makes me lie down in green pastures;
He leads me beside quiet waters.
He restores my soul;
He guides me in the paths of righteousness
For His name's sake.
Even though I walk through the valley of the shadow of death,
I fear no evil, for You are with me;
Your rod and Your staff, they comfort me.
You prepare a table before me in the presence of my enemies;
You have anointed my head with oil;
My cup overflows.
Surely goodness and lovingkindness
will follow me all the days of my life,
And I will dwell in the house of the Lord forever.[1]

A giant smile crashed through Judith's tears of joy, causing many people to stir from their grassy seats along the river's banks to make their own pilgrimage back to the God of their fathers. Her beloved, Abraham, was one of the first.

Judith's stirring song of love and worship to God made Abia suddenly self-aware of the condition of her heart. With Abia's crutch lying beside her on the rough, woven blanket where she sat and watched, she could not help but close her eyes and remember. Samuel had blamed himself for the accident; she had blamed the Roman soldier, and she held much bitterness toward him. The soldier stole from her the ability to walk, the ability to dance, the ability to marry, the ability to have children, and the ability to live a normal life. He had made her a cripple who had been ridiculed most of her life. Tears stung her eyes as Abia finally allowed the deep well of pain to rise up within her.

Abia was grateful in many ways for her life, but a life of what? Her heart was filled with hate, and it was stirred once again every time she saw a soldier or a galloping horse or heard any man except her father and brother laugh. Bitterness and resentment were constant, unwanted companions, and no matter how hard she tried, she could not make them leave. Abia finally realized she could not make them leave because she had invited them into her heart to stay through her sin of unforgiveness.

Added to bitterness and resentment toward the soldier was her sin of coveting the experiences of the people around her who could walk without crutches to lean on. They seemed to take for granted the amazing ability to walk without pain, and she secretly resented them for it. Jealously, Abia watched from the side those who danced at festivals and other celebrations. She even resented her own beloved sister, Judith, when she learned of her future marriage to Abraham and the children they would one day have. Shame and guilt relentlessly assaulted her, especially when she saw the sweet innocence of her sister as she came from the water only moments before.

Over and over again God had opened the path for the wayward nation of Israel to come back to the fold. But Abia's pride, shame, guilt, and mistaken belief that God owed her for the wrongs done to her by others kept her at arm's length from Him. She was no better than those from previous generations. Because Abia was only a five-year-old and an innocent victim when the incident left her lame, she later reckoned God owed her for the wrongs done to her by the soldier.

Abia had believed a lie.

How can I enjoy life and all the blessings of this life and not accept the trouble found in this life? Abia asked herself. *Worse still, how can I be angry with God when it was a man who sinned against me?* Opening her eyes, she saw the truth and desperately wanted to be washed of the filthiness left within her by any deed of darkness.

Despite a growing crowd of people urgently wanting to be baptized by John, John nevertheless, stopped to speak to Yaron. Yaron spoke something to Samuel, who dropped his head in humility. Ever so gently, Yaron and Samuel climbed the muddy bank toward Abia and brought her to John, the Wilderness Crier. John instructed them to seat Abia in the shallow running flow of water close to the shore. As she held his water-drenched arm and camel-haired sleeve, he leaned Abia backward until the cool cleansing water covered her whole body. "I baptize you with water, in preparation of the One coming. He will baptize you with holy fire," he said with confidence.

As Yaron and Samuel lifted Abia from the water's edge, Abia felt as if she could fly. Her heart was lighter than it had ever been before! God had heard the cry of her repentant heart that longed to be joined back with its Maker. Sin always separates—not God from His people, for His love is too great for that—but His people from a holy God.

After so many of her vain attempts to lick her wounds and rinse away her own sin-stained heart by valiant efforts and brave smiles, God had done what no person could do. He had cleansed what was inside the heart. Freedom, joy, and hope began to reverberate within Abia as never before.

CHAPTER 6

A Path Made Straight

The Ben-Davids' family studies of the Torah had taught them that, having been fashioned from the soil of the earth by the hands of God and given life by His own mouth, humankind was created as an earthly vessel made in God's likeness and image. Sin stained the cup of this vessel and made the soil of the earth dirty. John's wilderness cry pointed the way back to God, the Maker of the earthen vessel, just as Moses' message did centuries before.

People were created in the likeness of God and in the image of God, but were themselves not God. This baptism united Jews as a nation to once again turn from the belief that following Moses' Law meant they no longer needed the Messiah, no longer needed to wait for Him. The Law had been given as a way to show quite the opposite: a Savior was urgently needed. However, the Law soon became a graven image in the hearts of people. Those who felt they surpassed others in obeying the Law made themselves into graven images, believing they deserved to be worshiped and reverenced.

By adding to the Law, people, in essence, were eliminating others from becoming what they themselves desired: to be gods.

Those with repentant hearts, who had faith in the God of their fathers, were a remnant who desired to obey the Law as a form of worship to God. They understood there was no other God greater than Yahweh, least of all themselves. Yet, the Law was impossible to follow. It exhausted the strongest of people and defeated the wisest among them. It humbled the most prideful and filled the humble with hopelessness, causing them to cry out for God to save them from the Law.

They now realized that John was the messenger spoken of by the prophet Malachi—the one who would bring fellow Jews back to the Lord their God. His message included turning the hearts of the fathers to their children and the disobedient to the wisdom of the righteous and preparing the people for the Lord. He was called to baptize Jews to make them ritually and spiritually clean and ready for the Lord.

John's passionate message gave the Jews hope. Could it be this was a new beginning for the Jewish people? It certainly looked as though this was the first step toward restoration between human-kind and God. But the One who was coming after John would be more powerful and would complete the assignment. John was adamant with this message. John told the Jews that when the Messiah came He would teach them how to live and that all flesh would see the salvation of God. He taught that the new Kingdom of God was very near.

As the night fell and the stories ended in favor of some much needed sleep, the Ben-David family, like many others around Galilee, wondered if they would be the generation chosen to see the coming Messiah. No one ever imagined how very near He actually was.

CHAPTER 7

Bread and Gossip

The morning came quickly after a very short night to rest their aching backs and fingers from the seemingly endless sewing they had done the day before. The tea was black and hot, and the bread Hannah took from the oven brought to her family some measure of vitality. When breakfast was over and the cups were washed and put away, the family once again set about their work of sewing. About midmorning, Judith decided to take a turn at telling a story to relieve the humdrum of the constant stitching. It was one she experienced with Abraham, but had not had the opportunity to tell to her family, until now.

Judith's story began right after the Ben-David family was baptized in the Jordan River. Judith thoughtfully made a special embroidered handkerchief for her future mother-in-law, hoping the small gesture would bring her pleasure. She giggled when she divulged her secret desire to see her beloved, Abraham, and used the gift as an excuse to visit him. As the family diligently worked on their sewing assignments for the palace festival, Judith did not see the knowing glances exchanged by the rest of her family, who had known all along of her plans. Without looking up, she continued to tell her story. She had given Mora the gift, which was received with squeals of joy. Coming out of the bakery, Judith passed the new customer coming into the bakery and went to meet Abraham. He beckoned for her to sit with him on a bench outside the bakery, where he could get some fresh air away from the heat of the ovens.

Judith's future mother-in-law's voice traveled through the opened door, making conversation with Abraham almost impossible. With little else to do, they listened to the dialogue between Mora and the stranger. When Judith's own sister's name was mentioned, all efforts to talk with Abraham came to an end. Judith was accustomed to having her older sister discussed because of her disability, but being the loyal sister that she was, she needed to know what her future mother-in-law had to say.

"Abia, Abia? Oh, yes, I know her well," Mora, the baker's wife said, clucked in excitement, tasting an opportunity to share morsels of local gossip with the stranger who had come in for a loaf of freshly baked bread. "Tut, tut, tut," she exclaimed with a jerk of her head from side to side in a mixture of genuine sorrow and enthusiasm. "She is poor Yaron Ben-David and his wife's spinster daughter," she began her tale, inviting them both to sit down on the wooden bench that her husband had thoughtfully provided for the customers inside the bakery.

"Abia's younger sister Judith will soon be marrying my handsome son, Abraham," she cooed, as if the arrangement gave her liberty to tell what she knew to the stranger. "What a beautiful child Abia was, with her long, dark, flowing hair. She had brown eyes that always sparkled with mischief and a smile that charmed everyone, until the accident—it should have never happened," she said, looking up to Heaven, waiting for his disapproval. Finding none, she decided to continue. Drawing her muslin apron to her round, pudgy face, she wiped the sudden tears that left trenches down her flour-coated cheeks.

"Oy vey! A horrible day was that. The Roman soldier and his black, she-deviled horse came storming down the street. People had to scurry away as fast as they could to keep from being run down. Carts of wares spilled, poor things risking life and limb to pick up the messes. People were screaming trying to warn the people who were on down the street of the danger that was coming. Evil laughter filled the mouth of the soldier as he maneuvered his horse dangerously close to Samuel and his mule. It was for sport, I tell you; for sport! Samuel and his mule jumped from fright, poor things.

"It all happened so fast. The mule's head lifted, and its front feet danced high in the air, which made the cart's load shift and the cart tip over. There they were, poor creatures, Abia and her little sister, Judith. Playing under the cart they were. Their secret hiding place revealed. The Roman soldier's triumphant laugh drowned the whimpering cries of Samuel's dear sister, Abia, as her right hip was crushed beneath the cart. Three-year-old Judith cried unhurt as her five-year-old sister's life was changed forever," the baker's wife said.

"Time heals old pain, while it creates new ones," she whispered, as if mentioning the event would superstitiously cause mishap to her or her family. "For 12 long years Samuel, her brother, has been consumed with guilt since it was discovered that poor Abia, God help her, could do nothing with her leg but schlep it behind her as she tried to walk. My sweet daughter, Sarah, was so in love with Samuel at the time, but of course could not wait until Samuel was free of his responsibility."

Mora smiled with her mouth, but resentment flowed from her eyes as she remembered how another husband had to be found for Sarah after she had been rejected by Samuel.

Considering the rejection as an insult to the whole family, Mora did not know what to do. The two families had been friends for many years. Yet, her family had been embarrassed by the event, and Mora was very leery when Abraham, her only son, was pledged to be married to Samuel's littlest sister, Judith. Mora seemed afraid that Judith might do to Abraham what her brother did to Sarah. Did she think it was a family illness passed among the Ben-David siblings?

Piously, Mora told the stranger how excited she was to have Judith be her daughter and delivered proof of her claim by showing the stranger the lovely handkerchief Judith had gifted her with, as though it were proof of Judith's commitment to marry her son, Abraham.

"Enough about me," she said demurely, "You did ask about Abia, after all."

Mora continued the story as if she had never stopped. "And that ugly crutch she has to use, more's the pity for the poor child. Abia had to learn to face head-on the unkind stares of the people who watched her stumble with a wooden crutch. Her dark eyes are somewhat dulled by the constant pain, you know, but her smile still has the power to charm the most curious. She has learned to cry behind her smile, as all Jewish women learn to do."

"The hardest of all to face is the conclusions some people make that it was God Himself judging her and that the accident was a sign or proof of some hidden family sin."

Mora hid from the stranger her puzzled eyes that still held the same question of suspicion. But that could not possibly be, she had reckoned, because Abraham, her fine boy, was to marry the youngest daughter from the same family. She reasoned that Judith was a strong girl and would bring to the family many handsome sons.

"The Ben-Davids had always fared well by their ability to sew incredible works of art and had made quite a name for themselves, yet this terrible tragedy…! Who can understand the workings of God?" She continued, "Abia is 17 now; her unfortunate parents cannot find her a husband, for who but her own family would want her? What is certain is certain. Neither a wife nor a mother could she be, poor girl." Her mouth muttered a quick, self-satisfied prayer of thanksgiving for the recent marriage of her other rather homely daughter of 17, Agatha.

Mora remembered the stranger. "How this old woman rambles on and on, please forgive me," her face flushed from sudden embarrassment and guilt of sharing such intimate details of her close friend Hannah's child to this man, this stranger.

"Do I know you? You look somehow very familiar to me," she purred softly, swiftly turning back to her favorite vice, gossip.

"No, you do not know Me yet," He said with hidden meaning. "I cannot stay any longer for I am late to see my cousin. I pray we will get to know each other one day very soon," He said with sincerity.

With that said, the stranger tucked His bread purchase in the crook of His arm. His eyes danced with merriment as He turned to make his way out of doors, leaving her with myriad unanswered questions starting to form in her mind.

"But kind sir, I did not catch Your name." She pleaded for a morsel of information to pass along to other customers who might visit her later in the day.

Just when she thought He did not hear her question, He turned to her with a humble smile and said, "My name is Jesus." With a nod of His head toward Judith and Abraham, who were still sitting on the bench in front of the bakery, He disappeared into the crowded marketplace on His way to meet His cousin, John, at the river's edge.

"My future mother-in-law is a misplaced soul who was orphaned as a young girl and was passed around from one family member to another. Her tongue often reflects her wounds and inner struggles. Mora's loving family is very patient with her and so must I be," the maturity in which Judith spoke seemed beyond her 15 years.

"Mora is a actually a bighearted woman, but her fear of rejection causes her to act out in ways that often hurt others. I have tried to show her acts of kindness, and she has grown to love me, and I have grown to love her, too," Judith said, reassuring her family of her future happiness.

"I took the handkerchief to her to show her kindness and to see Abraham," explained Judith with a smile, "But more importantly, dear family, that is how I first met Jesus!"

CHAPTER 8

The Aftermath
of Prophetic Destinies
When They Collide

Excitement grew even greater when John, the Baptizer, spoke of the coming Messiah. He indicated the time would not be very long until the Messiah would come to His beloved people. John said he would identify Him. The Jewish people had waited for centuries for the Jewish Messiah. Could it be that He would come to this generation?

One day can look like another, but amazingly, as the sun sets, history can be made within that ordinary period of time. On one such day, a man named Jesus joined others who were gathered awaiting baptism. He requested of John to baptize Him in the Jordan River.

When John looked up from the muddy water and saw Jesus, John the Wilderness Crier suddenly became John the Messiah Revelator. "Behold, the Lamb of God who takes away the sins of the world!" John proclaimed with great enthusiasm.

The distinction of being chosen to announce the Messiah to the world was overwhelming. John dropped to his knees in the muddy banks of the Jordan in humility and declared his unworthiness to baptize Jesus when he was asked to do so. With humility and a gentle smile, Jesus raised John from his kneeling place and encouraged him to fulfill his destiny.

When John baptized Jesus, the sky miraculously split apart. From the heavens above, the Holy Spirit took on the bodily form of a dove that landed on Jesus. A powerful voice came from the heavenly Father and said, "You are My Beloved Son; I am well-pleased with You." Not since the world's creation had God the Father, God the Son, and God the Holy Spirit appeared on Earth together until that moment.

The reports of the divine manifestations caused a great disturbance within the region, especially to the religious leaders. Some people claimed the noise was only natural rumbles of thunder in the skies, while others heard clearly the voice of God the Father and watched the Holy Spirit in the form of a dove land on Jesus' shoulder. Hearing something unusual caused others to deduce the sound was indeed a proclamation of God. They believed He was calling special attention to the baptism that took place that day between John and Jesus. Only some argued the special attention paid by God showed His displeasure, while others believed it was His affirmation.

Many people shook their heads, rejecting the whole event. Declaring all the people involved as crazy or delusional, they threw away all explanations with one wave of their self-righteous hands.

A delegation of religious men was formed, and they set out to investigate this preposterous claim that Jesus was the Messiah. They wanted proof that they were right in their opinion: the whole event was too impossible. Closed-minded, they already knew the answers to any and all questions posed. Knowing the Holy Scriptures as they did, it became easy for them to find fault and incriminating evidence against anything remotely positive about the circumstance. Their ultimate goal became to discredit and harm the reputations of John and Jesus at the same time. They questioned with doubt and uncertainty to explain away those things their faith was not developed enough to handle.

There were also a growing number of people who asked questions for the purpose of genuinely requesting information on the matter. They posed the questions to debate, to ponder, to look for clues and details for consideration. Looking for all possible conclusions or points of view, they weighed all the possibilities, both pro and con, before coming to a decision.

Whatever the reason for the questions, some questions only developed into more questions. Why did John not recognize Jesus as the Son of God until the baptism? Could it be that John did not understand that Jesus was the true Messiah until Jesus' baptism, when his own eyes beheld the Holy Spirit come from a split in the heavens? Could it be that when he saw that, he was able to see more? Could it be his own faith increased when he saw the Holy Spirit for himself? Was it significant for John when the Holy Spirit took the form of a dove and landed on Jesus? Could it be the Holy Spirit is powerful and can share with humankind great mysteries of God? Could the Holy Spirit have recognized Jesus not only as the Messiah, but also as the Passover Lamb, and have supernaturally imparted this knowledge to John?

People were frantically searching for answers to life's woes and were excited when they heard John speak out against injustice in all its forms. They trusted him. But to lay claim to the idea that his cousin was the Son of God was quite another thing entirely. The suspicious were certain the whole thing was a family scheme to gain position and power by tricking those who were unaware and uneducated. Disbelief and hope both spread rapidly with each passing day. More and more turmoil was arising in the district, making it unsafe for everyone, especially Jesus and His cousin John.

CHAPTER 9

And It Came to Pass

"Yaron, my old friend! So this is where you have been keeping yourself," Malachi shouted from the common courtyard outside the kitchen room as he made his way indoors—as he had done for as long as any one of them could remember. Yaron stood from his chair in honor of the older man who had been a good friend and neighbor of the Ben-David family longer than Yaron had been alive.

"Come! Come in, my old friend!" Yaron said as he beckoned Malachi to take the padded chair he had just vacated, preferring the harder one for himself.

"If Moses will not come to the mountain, the mountain must come to Moses!" this old Jewish man's voice shook with laughter, leaving no doubt that his joke was meant to convey how much he missed his younger friend Yaron at his regular booth in the marketplace. For many years, the two of them had spent many hours together drinking dark tea as they shared their views on politics and religion with each other. Yaron's own father, long since deceased, had looked upon Malachi as a father figure, but he was also his closest friend.

Malachi's hand shook like his voice as he accepted the dark tea Hannah offered him as he took his seat among the family. Malachi had been a vital part of the Ben-David family ever since the time when his wife and only son—who was four years old—were killed by the cruel hands of the Roman soldiers when they searched far and wide for the newborn King of the Jews some almost 30 years ago. Yaron was 17 at the time and had just lost his little brother by the same fate. Soon afterword, Yaron's parents began often inviting Malachi over for meals since he had vowed to never take another wife as a result of his overwhelming grief and guilt for having not been home to save his wife and child. Yaron and Malachi's unique friendship developed slowly, and somehow the relationship seemed to ease each other's pain.

"Please, do not stop your work for this old man," he said referring to himself. "I have heard of the great honor you have been given to sew for Herod's birthday celebration," the old man said, with a trace of bitterness in his voice that arose whenever he had the occasion to speak of the house of Herod. "Jewish workmanship is far superior to anything the Romans could ever muster, and your work will honor us all." His loyalty to faith and family was paramount and had grown despite all the trials and tribulations he had faced throughout the years. He was old, but his mind was sharp, and he possessed an uncanny ability to make sense of their world that seemed, at times, to be nothing but chaos to others.

"I am very interested in the man named John who has come from the wilderness, and his cousin named Jesus. There is something in the air and public opinions and viewpoints about these two men that make the air thick with controversy and much debate," he said. Malachi, an excellent storyteller, brought much relief to the family as they laboriously worked on the fabric designs. As he settled into his chair, enjoying the company of this family that he considered his own, he began his story of historical events that he personally had lived through and shared his own beliefs and opinions. As he spoke, threads from the past and threads of the present were woven together, bringing forth a tapestry picture of the times in which they lived as seen through the eyes of an old Jewish man.

John and Jesus' family connection was being discussed at great length in the marketplace and was cause for a growing number of heated discussions. Some insisted John to be the Messiah while others maintained Jesus to be the Messiah. A third more popular group supported neither claim, but was not to be left out of the interesting intellectual debate.

John's mother, Elizabeth, at an old age had become pregnant with John, just as the angel Gabriel had prophesied. Elizabeth kept herself in seclusion for five months. She was thankful to God for extending His favor upon her and taking away the disgrace her barrenness had been to her and others. Perhaps, like Sarah and Hannah from Israel's past, she had remained barren because God had a greater plan for her. Could it be that her barren state would heighten the sense that her impending pregnancy was indeed a great miracle?

When Elizabeth was in her sixth month, her cousin Mary, who was also from Aaron's priestly lineage, was also visited by God's angel. Mary was told that she was chosen to bear a son, Jesus, whom the Holy Spirit of God conceived in her although she was a virgin. Jesus would be great and would be called the Son of the Most High and heir to the ancient throne of David. Mary gave permission by saying to the angel, "I am the handmaiden of the Lord. May it be to me just as you have said."

Mary was betrothed to Joseph with a formal witnessed agreement made legally binding between Mary and Joseph's families. The bride's price had been paid to Mary's family, and they were to be formally married about a year later; but until then, she remained in the home of her parents. When Mary revealed that she was expecting a baby and Joseph was not the father, it created a great scandal, especially since the bride's price had already been paid.

An honor killing of his fiancée, Mary, by Joseph's family was well within their rights and was expected. Instead, Joseph sent Mary away to visit Elizabeth, who lived about a hundred miles away in Judea. Hoping to save her from this fate, he wanted to get her out of the way until a solution could be worked out.

When Elizabeth, who was still pregnant with John, greeted her cousin Mary, the baby in her womb moved and was suddenly was filled with the Holy Spirit. In a moment of penetrating spiritual clarity, Elizabeth recognized she was being visited by the mother of the expected Messiah. She pronounced a blessing on her young cousin saying, "Blessed are you among women, and blessed is the fruit of your womb. And why has this happened to me that the mother of my Lord comes to me? For as soon as I heard the sound of your greeting, the child in my womb leaped for joy. And blessed is she who believed that there would be a fulfillment of what was spoken to her by the Lord."

Mary stayed with her older cousin and other loving and concerned relatives and friends who came to share in the joyous occasion with Elizabeth until she gave birth to her son John. Meanwhile, Joseph was said to have had a dream from God verifying the truth of Mary's pregnancy story: she was carrying the child of God within her.

After John's birth, Mary left Elizabeth's house and went back to Joseph, who took her as his wife. Having heard from God in the dream, he was not afraid to do so. He dreamed that the child conceived in her was of the Holy Spirit and that his name was to be called Jesus because He would save His people from their sins. The young couple went away to Bethlehem for a census that was being taken by Caesar Augustus, the first Roman emperor in charge of Judea.

While they were there, Mary gave birth to her firstborn son in a dark, dirty, and smelly stable because the town was filled and there was no more room to be found at the inn. It was not quite the royal surroundings the Messiah King should be born in, but it seemed to be God's plan.

Out in the fields where shepherds looked out over their flock by night, the angel Gabriel appeared yet again and declared the good news with great joy that in the city of David a savior was born. The shepherds went to visit the child who was wrapped in swaddling clothes. God was with His people once again—Immanuel, "God with us"—in the form of a newborn baby. The night sky filled with heavenly hosts who praised God for the birth of His Son, the Prince of Peace.

Guided by a star in the heavens, Magi, or wise men from the East, found Mary, Joseph, and the baby Jesus in Bethlehem. They worshiped Him there and gave gifts for the newborn King.

Already extremely suspicious and fearful, King Herod was greatly alarmed that a takeover by the religious people of Judea would occur. He believed that if they rallied around a newborn Jewish king he would be stripped of the title "king of the Jews." Herod tried to trick the Magi into revealing to him the child's whereabouts, but was unsuccessful. He sent his soldiers out to find the child, but did not find him. Herod wanted to intimidate and frighten the people of Judah, so all very young male children in Bethlehem and surrounding regions were slaughtered.

The pain in Malachi's voice was evident as he spoke. No Jew in the region at that time was unaffected by the tragedy. Knowing the mere mentioning of this time in their history would cause everyone's wounds to be opened, he quickly continued on with his story.

Elizabeth took John to the wilderness area of Judea and did everything as the Lord had instructed her. Some say she went there to escape from Herod's wrath because John, who was under the age of two, was in great danger as well. She went alone. It was rumored that King Herod, in a fit of jealous rage and unsubstantiated suspicions, had Zachariah slain. Some said Herod's insanity was so great he even believed the old priest Zachariah was the newborn King of the Jews. Others reported that story was fabricated as a front for the real truth: Zachariah was killed for defying Herod's soldiers and sending his wife away in the wilderness to save his own son from imminent doom. Others said Zachariah was killed as a result of refusing to reveal the whereabouts of another Jewish boy, his own nephew, Jesus, and was rewarded with punishment for insubordination. Miraculously, John and Jesus both lived.

Having been warned in another dream, Joseph took Mary and Jesus to Egypt to escape the danger of Herod's edict and remained there until Herod's death, when it was safe to return to Israel. Finally settling in a city called Nazareth, Jesus grew in stature and in favor with people and God until the time of His baptism by John.

John and Jesus were now both 30 years old, but the events of their births were greatly impacting the lives of those who encountered either one of them. Like wind on cinders, it ignited a flame of passionate responses from the truth seekers and fury in the hearts of others who deemed them as charlatans, swindlers, and blasphemers.

John had already made fierce enemies of the leading and most prominent religious leaders who had come to the Jordan River with the pretense of wanting to be baptized. Although he held no power or position in the Jewish political, economical, or religious systems, John spoke with great authority and told the highly religious they were sinful. Calling them a "brood of vipers," he confronted them and challenged their sincerity. He said true repentance would bear good fruit and that they could not excuse away their sinful behavior on the grounds of their rich ancestry, nor could they rely on the faith of their fathers. Pointing to the sinful behaviors and conduct of the extremely religious made him enemies all around, but John pressed onward in his destiny and calling despite the rumors of threats of bodily harm and even death plots.

From the shores of the Jordan River, John spoke openly of social and religious injustices to the large numbers of people who gathered along its banks. He also openly criticized Roman interference in ruling the people of God. This included the family of Herod, who were not of Jewish descent and, in fact, had murdered many Jewish rabbis.

It was reported that when Herod heard some of the reports coming from the Jordan River about John the Baptist, he requested an audience with him. Herod enjoyed talking with John because he considered him strange and very unlike anyone he had met before. Over a period of time, he came to think John to be a holy man, despite John's criticism of him for marrying Herodias when his first wife was not dead. John and many others considered their marriage one of adultery according to the laws of God, believing she divorced herself from her first husband to marry Herod, but did not obtain a legal divorce from him. There was also concern that Herod Antipas had an unnatural relationship with his niece, Salome, when she came to live with him after he married her mother. All these beliefs were foreign to Herod, although he considered himself to be a Jew. He admired the boldness and bravado of John to utter such things in his presence.

Herodias, on the other hand, was incensed. How dare he criticize them, his own sovereigns? What impudence for John to speak of royal matters among the peasants of the region. To then have the nerve to judge the royal couple as sinful in the eyes of their God and offensive to the Jewish people was simply not heard of. Her resentment of John grew hourly. As soon as possible, she put extreme pressure on Antipas to have John arrested and put into prison at Herod's palace.

Malachi was exhausted from the long conversation with Yaron and the rest of his family. "For a man of little words and one whose old legs do not work as the once did, you certainly have an ear to the pulse of the community!"

Yaron's gentle teasing was not missed by the old man, who responded in kind. "Between you and me, the problems of this world could be solved quite easily! I will take my leave, but will pay you a visit again soon. My old legs need the exercise, but for now there is a soft bed that seems to be needing me," Malachi said with a smile as he referred to the nap he had grown accustomed to taking every afternoon.

As Malachi slowly made his way home, Yaron and the family discussed all of the things he shared. They greatly admired the wisdom of the older man. With the additional information he had given them about what he knew of John and his cousin, Jesus, they had much food for thought and further discussion. The drama that was unfolding daily around them had many players, and the plot was getting more involved with each passing day.

Meanwhile, Jesus went to a desert area near where John had spent his formative years. Being led by the Holy Spirit of God, Jesus fasted and then was tempted by the devil. For 40 days He was with wild beasts and faced the full wrath of satan.

It was widely believed that satan, or lucifer, had once been the highly acclaimed one who had ministered to God in Heaven, but through an act of disobedience, he rebelled against God. He despised God and resented Him for creating the man called Adam, who was made in the image and likeness of God. Adam was created different from other living creatures created by God. Adam had God's ability to reproduce and create life like animals, but with an incredible distinction: God's own image, likeness, and distinctive characteristics could be passed from one generation to the next.

Lucifer considered that the Father had replaced him and all angels with His new creation, and he vowed to get even. This came to a head when he received word that God was walking in a special garden called Eden with this man named Adam and his wife, Eve. Lucifer became obsessed with jealousy. Given free will, just as humankind was given, lucifer sinned against God. Now power hungry and possessed with the desire to lash back at God the Father, lucifer vowed in his heart to destroy humankind. Lucifer was dismissed from Heaven, and he took a third of the angelic host with him. He furiously came to the conclusion that if he could influence humankind to sin as he had done, he would be rid of the source of his contention. By doing so, he could inject the Father with the same pain he believed God had inflicted on him when He created humans.

In the Garden of Eden, Adam and Eve were influenced by satan to sin and rebel against God by eating the only fruit in the whole Garden they had been forbidden by God to eat. It was a hoax, ploy, trick, and deception; yes, but they were rebellious nonetheless. God had equipped Adam and Eve with free choice of their wills, having already proven to them how magnificently He could take care of all their needs. Earth was created for them as was all that the earth provided. God supplied them with everything. He was their God, and they were His people to rule and reign over the earth. Making them stewards of His Kingdom on Earth, He instructed them to be fruitful and multiply and fill and subdue the earth. The Garden of Eden was a place blessed by God. One kernel of corn produced an ear of corn with endless more corn. Sowing corn reaped a harvest of corn.

After their rebellion, God had to remove Adam and Eve because the same law of sowing and reaping was in effect. By making the choice from free will, they planted seeds of pride, rebellion, doubt, and suspicion of God instead of worship of the Creator. Sin planted in the fertile soil found in The Garden would reap a huge harvest of sin. Adam and Eve had worshiped the created being, satan, and followed him instead of God, so Father had no choice but to remove them from The Garden they once shared. When sin entered The Garden, sin's evil consequences would also be reaped with endless possibilities of evil.

Satan won a victory by Adam and Eve's rebellion against God. Sin entered the earth and was multiplied. Dominion over the earth and people was handed to satan.

When God slaughtered an innocent lamb to cover Adam and Eve's nakedness, He made a blood covenant with them. One day He would send One who would cover their sins, forgive the sins, and restore their relationship once again back to their Father.

The Father waited for the right time in history when He would execute the plan foretold in The Garden. The Father would provide a second Adam to win back His people from satan. Conceived by the power of the Holy Spirit, Jesus the Son of God would enter the womb gate of Mary. Fully man and fully God, Jesus would do what the first Adam could not do.

When satan found out about Jesus' birth, he went about trying to kill Him through Herod the Great and other agents of evil on Earth. Failing in the attempt, he decided to put Him to the test to prove Jesus was fully human. Jesus needed no such proof, but satan did.

Jesus had been baptized to wash away the sins of the first Adam. Preparing Him for His ministry, the Holy Spirit filled Him and the Father validated Him. The temptation in the desert required the Son of God to not use any rights or privileges of His deity.

Three temptation scenarios were offered to Jesus, each unmasking the tactics satan held over humankind. The first was an attempt to give in to the temptation of pride and prove to satan who Jesus really was. It dealt with lust of the flesh, sinful humanity's cravings, and primitive desires. The next one dealt with an offering for power and wealth, which ultimately led to satan's desire for Jesus to worship him by kissing his feet. Lust of the eyes and greedy ambitions were at its root. Last was the temptation to be worshiped and praised above God, to have popularity and public recognition.

With each of the three temptations, Jesus fought satan not by divine powers, but by the ones the Spirit and the Word of God possessed. Jesus then ordered satan away with words that must have stung him, "You must worship the Lord your God and serve only Him." With that said, satan left, and the angels came and took care of Jesus.

When Jesus returned from the desert after 40 days, He heard that John the Baptist had been put into prison. Jesus then left Nazareth and went to live in Capernaum near Lake Galilee. He started to preach, saying that one's heart had to be changed to bring about changes in one's life. This change was vital because the Kingdom of Heaven was near.

Jesus picked 12 men who stayed with Him, and He made disciples of them. Jesus went everywhere in Galilee, teaching in the synagogues, preaching the Good News about the Kingdom of Heaven, and healing all the people's diseases and sicknesses. The news about Jesus spread all over the region.

A few days later, Malachi returned to tell Yaron and his family more of the story of Jesus' activities. Malachi reported that Jesus was trying to edify and built up the people who had become weary trying to obey the Law and the exaggerated human-made laws that accompanied it. "Do to others what you want them to do to you. This is the meaning of the Law of Moses and the teaching of the prophets," He told them.

His teachings were simple and about practical everyday things, like how to deal with anger, divorce, making rash promises or oaths, worship, giving, and prayer. He showed the people how to ask God for what they need and how to be careful of money's importance. "People know you by your actions and your words," He advised. It would be difficult to follow these principles, but the rewards would be worth it.

People everywhere were following Jesus around and were eye-witnesses to Jesus healing a man with leprosy. They saw a soldier's servant being healed when Jesus was not even with him. And they witnessed Jesus healing a demonized man, too. People saw the great healings, but as often happens, many criticized what they could not understand. Some started saying that demons obeyed Jesus because He was a demon Himself.

The Pharisees and Sadducees took full advantage of the grow-ing sense of unrest Jesus was provoking, especially when He talked about being the Son of God. The people started to argue about Jesus. Some said, "He is a prophet," while others said, "He is the Christ." People tried to capture Him, and the Temple guards were ordered to arrest Him.

Jesus visited the synagogue at His hometown of Nazareth. To the rabbi and congregation He read a passage from the prophet Isaiah, chapter 61 verses 1 and 2:

The Spirit of the Lord God is upon me, because the Lord has anointed me to bring good news to the afflicted; He has sent me to bind up the brokenhearted, to proclaim liberty to captives, and freedom to prisoners; to proclaim the favorable year of the Lord...

Then He said that those words were being fulfilled that day. Many were astonished and highly upset that He could be pro-claiming Himself to be the Messiah.

Yet He spoke with such confidence and authority that many believed Jesus to be the Messiah. Jesus did not seem like the king many were expecting, but everyone who knew His healing touch was drawn to Him by the incredible love in His eyes. He offered an acceptance that penetrated the heart and caused many people to love and serve Him. It seemed strange that the very things that caused some to love Him caused others to hate Him.

CHAPTER 10

"My Dancer"

Jesus. His name was certainly causing a stir. Skeptics, truth seekers, and the curious could be found daily in search of Him. The marketplace was becoming filled with the talk of His ability to heal the lame and sick among them. Wherever Jesus moved, crowds began to gather, hoping to be ones Jesus would touch or speak to. So many of the people who had been healed were relatives or friends of the Ben-David family. Knowing of their great suffering, everyone was elated when the report came that they had been healed and set free at of the hands of Jesus.

As the evening was settling in and the sun at long last was nestled into the western sky, the ending of another day of sewing was at hand. After their dinner, Hannah and her daughter, Abia stepped outside to enjoy the beautifully colored sky as the sun left its final mark on the day.

Hannah was thankful to be able to once again stand up instead of having to sit all of the time to sew. As her thoughts traveled to the time before Abia was healed, it became fresh and anew to her how difficult it must have been for Abia to be stranded in one place for long periods of time without being able to get any form of relief from the pain it caused. With her daughter's accident on her mind, she wanted to hear once again the story about how her pain had ended.

Without knowing it, mother and daughter had the same thoughts. Abia was still amazed, realizing how wonderful it was to be able to rise from a sitting position without assistance and walk without the assistance of a crutch.

"My dear daughter, tell me again the story of the day when you first met Jesus," her mother implored Abia. "I will never grow tired of hearing it, and I thank God for every remembrance of that special time."

"The tale really began when I was four years old with a series of dreams about a nice young man who encouraged me to dance. Do you remember, Momma?" Abia inquired.

With a nod of her head, Hannah acknowledged the time period Abia was referring to. "Yes, I remember the dreams well. The first one that came true was about your accident, and the other dreams about dancing did not seem at all possible at the time. Yet, look at you my daughter, you are healed and whole! I know you suffered greatly, and if the the past is still too pain-filled, do not tell it," Hannah said with compassion she had learned from tending to her invalid daughter for 12 years.

"Yes, we have all suffered, but I am healed and whole, as you have said. It is my desire to tell the story again and again only with the hope of giving glory to God and to possibly give hope to the hopeless among us." With a grateful heart, Abia began to recount her story to her mother.

It had begun about a year before when, one afternoon, Abia's best friend, Mary, was sitting with her under the shade of an awning that Yaron had made long ago for Mary's father, who was a shoemaker. Yaron had traded the awning for a pair of shoes made especially for Abia with extra thick soles. Her shoes were prone to wear out quickly from dragging one foot when she walked, and those shoes lasted longer than most.

"Go, Abia, go to Him. Maybe you will be healed," Mary advised her friend when she heard Jesus was only a short distance from her home. "He is only just coming, Abia. Samuel will take you. You know he will if you ask him," she pleaded, giving automatic answers for every possible objection Abia might have.

Mary had already confided in Abia about her interest in Samuel. Mary's continual questions about him every time the two friends talked was a giveaway of the growing emotions she had for him. Keeping her secret from Samuel was very difficult for Abia, especially when Samuel had made the same confession to her about Mary. The prospect of Samuel someday marrying Mary made her extremely excited. She would love for her brother to find his true love, and she trusted Mary with his heart and would love to have her in the family.

Mary looked up just at the moment that Samuel was walking by. "Samuel, Abia has something to ask of you," Mary sweetly informed him, forcing Abia to make a quick decision.

With a roll of the eyes toward Mary, Abia asked Samuel, if he was not too busy, if he would possibly take her for a ride in the cart to follow Jesus, who was fast approaching.

Before she knew what was happening, she was loaded onto the cart and was heading down the dusty road that was swelling with people who were looking for Jesus to heal them or who wanted to listen to one of His wonderful teachings.

Samuel was leading the mule that was carrying Abia when he stopped for people to pass in front of them. Abia's head was spinning, and suddenly she became afraid. Her mind swam with questions. *What if He has already passed? What if He is too busy or cannot see me for the throngs of people who are lining the dirt street? What if He does see me and walks in our direction?* Just as she was about to indicate to Samuel her change of heart and her desire to go back home, Samuel smiled and greeted Jesus, who had walked around the back of the cart to its front.

Thankful for the veil that covered her face, Abia watched Jesus make the short distance toward her and then appear on the right side of her. He touched Abia's hand with His to get her attention. Bowing from His waist, very properly, He whispered, "My dancer."

A sudden wave of self-pity rolled over Abia, causing her heart to fill with pain that her eyes could not hide. In a flash, the walls surrounding her heart stood at attention as she tried to hide her eyes from His penetrating ones. *Can He not see I am unable to walk? Is this some kind of joke?*

Not sure what she was drawn to first, His generous smile or the look she saw in His dark brown eyes—and deciding it was probably both—Abia permitted herself to look at Him. There was something very familiar about Him, but she could not identify it.

"My dancer," He had called her. *Was He making fun of me or was He reading my heart's cry?* How did He know? Looking into His eyes for the brief moment after He spoke, Abia honesty saw nothing but love, with no hint of cruelty. The look in His eyes seemed to be some kind of encouragement. They seemed to invoke hope and trust. It was as though He was pleading with her to believe in Him and His words. Deep within His stare, He challenged her not to doubt what He was declaring when He called her His dancer.

Dancing was what Abia missed more than anything else. It was the unspoken desire of her heart. She longed for the days before her accident when she twirled around and around in childish abandon. Like all children, she had danced, but it was much more to her than just child's play. She seemed to sense a closeness to God when she danced that she could not explain. Even her name, Abia, meant "worshiper of God." *How could Jesus know what no one else in the world knew?*

Suddenly dreams from the past about dancing raced through her mind. She had been warned in one of the dreams about an accident that left her moaning words like playing, soldier, leg, and hurts. And indeed, the dream had come true.

Ever since the tragedy, her thoughts had been consumed with dance. Obediently, she had followed the advice of a doctor, who insisted that the best way for her to have any hope of walking was to lie on her back for months so her hip and leg bones could mend. Her mission was to do everything humanly possible in the hopes of being able to sit, stand, walk, and one day dance again.

Day after day, night after night, the pain had been relentless. Suffering came in many forms—liniments that burned her skin and other remedies that did nothing, yet promised to do the miraculous. Soon misery and self-pity replaced many of her childhood friends, who would come to see her with picked flowers, but then run back to their homes. Sorrow danced with tears as grief partnered with heartache and the reality of her injuries took their toll.

When at long last the day had come for her to sit up in her bed, the pain had been unbearable because she had been immobile for such a long time. Hot towels for her hip made the process easier. When at last she could stand, one leg bore full weight while the other danced lifelessly beside it. The driving force behind every setback and every painful experience was her hope and will to dance again.

As weeks rolled into months and months into years, Abia gradually began to make progress in walking with the aid of a wooden crutch that Samuel had carved from a wooden stick. He padded the top and instructed her on how to use it in place of the lame leg and lean on it for support. Tears of joy danced in the eyes of Abia's entire family when at long last she took her first steps with her crutch as a new partner.

Consumed with the hope and desire to dance, Abia had taken advantage of being alone one afternoon while everyone was outside in the courtyard. She stood up with the aid of her crutch and began to pray for God to help her and cause her to be able to dance as she once had done so easily. Leaning on the crutch, she began to sway from side to side to a rhythm resounding in her head. Casting caution to the wind and the crutch away from her side, she landed in a heap upon the floor—along with all of her hopes of dancing. Tears of frustration marched down her cheeks as her mind assessed any bodily damages from the fall. Facts were facts: she could not physically dance. It was a bitter pill to swallow.

Abia also remembered the dream she once had about trying to dance with Momma's broomstick. Finding it too difficult, she opted to walk with it instead. She was realizing that indeed that dream had come true as well.

With little else to do, Abia had danced in her mind and pondered its importance and looked for its significance. The accident had left her without the ability to dance or have full range of movement, but there was something more than movement that she longed for. To dance was important, but why?

At five years old, she had been too young to search for the deeper meaning of dance. As she reflected upon the earlier times, Abia began to gain some understanding. As a young child, dancing had been simply a means to bring her joy and a way to express what was in her heart.

As time passed, she began to watch her younger sister for many years express her emotions through dance. Skipping, jumping, turning, and spinning in circles conveyed delight, while stomps could convey displeasure or frustration. Having witnessed many of Judith's emotions expressed through dance, Abia also saw how it communicated to others her emotions without her uttering a word. Her silent form of communication also brought forth a response from those who observed it. The former brought smiles and applause, while the latter brought forth a disapproving, raised eyebrow or a quick smack on the behind.

For 12 years Abia pondered what dance meant to her and whether it could have a greater purpose than merely expressing one's childish emotions. Despite having all capability to personally engage in dance stripped from her, it completely occupied Abia's thoughts. This was a mystery to her, yet she was driven by a strong need or inner compulsion to find its secrets. When she heard how Zachariah had been struck dumb as a sign to others of his divine encounter with an angel of the Lord, Abia realized that God's ways are quite different from hers. Zachariah's silence actually spoke to others. It became a communication tool in the hands of God.

In the hands of God, could dance be used for communication purposes? As Abia remembered dancing when she was young, she realized she had been communicating with God in an extremely unique way. Her body and mind spoke silent worship messages to Him, which He understood. What was even more amazing was that her dancing also invoked a response from Him! Abia had an inner knowing of what pleased Him and that dancing was what she was created for.

With one problem solved, another filled its place. If dance is a tool to be used as a means of communication, then what else is it? Dance as a tool was a new concept. As she knew it, a tool was something that could be used as a means of achieving a desired result or for accomplishing a particular purpose. A needle was a tool she was very familiar with. A sewing needle in the hands of a tailor can be skillfully used to produce the desired result or purpose of a lovely warm coat for winter or a sturdy sail for fishing.

In the hands of the Creator, could dance be used to accomplish something beyond communication? Is it possible that He could use dance movements to accomplish something on Earth that He desired? Could the dancer be a tool in His hand for His purposes to be fulfilled? Could the dancer and the dance illustrate to others God's particular intentions here on Earth and with His power make them happen? Abia's questions seemed as endless as her desire to dance—and equally as hopeless.

Recalling dreams from the past that involved dancing, she was reminded of how they were used to awaken something inside her. *Was I destined to dance? Was God speaking to me through my dreams to point the way for me?* But that was a long time ago before the circumstances of her life had put an abrupt stop to all hope of seeing her destiny fulfilled. She had stopped having the dreams about dance when she reached the age of six.

The reality of Abia's deformed hip and leg, which had replaced the perfectly healthy ones in her dreams, was too painful. The sweet memory of the wonderful dreams of dancing with the very nice man had grown dim with each passing year. All hope of feeling His hand in hers once more as they danced in the streets of Jerusalem had dissolved. Gone was the special language He taught her to speak when she danced with Him; the loud voice of disillusionment and discouragement had replaced it. The delightful little tune He once sang to her in her dreams had long faded. It was replaced with new dirges of lamenting and sadness as she mourned the unfulfilled dreams of dance within her.

With a quick shake of her head, she forced her thoughts from the past back to the present. Once again Abia heard the voices of the crowds who were gathering to find Jesus. He stood patiently before her, allowing her time to process what the statement "My dancer" had awakened within her. His dark brown eyes seemed to convey how much He understood her conclusions of defeat and hopelessness, but they showed no signs of condemnation.

Leaning toward her, He once again whispered the words, "My dancer." With that said, He turned and slowly walked away. Soon He disappeared in the growing masses of people who lined the road in desperate need of His healing touch.

Just then, Abia heard the faint sound of Him whistling as He departed. There it was again! She had heard that tune before, but where? When? Suddenly she remembered! It was the tune sung by the man in her dreams when they walked down the streets of Jerusalem, and He healed all the people who reached out to Him.

Joy rose up within her. Could she dare hope again? Could she dare believe that her dreams could come true? It was baffling to her to have such joy when her lifeless leg remained hidden under the dusty riding blanket and the ugly wooden crutch was close at hand. Yet, there it was. Hope, as impossible as it seemed, soared through her mind and her heart for the first time since her accident.

As Abia heard the sound of the whistle grow fainter, she felt optimism rise. She could not comprehend it or explain it, but she felt she could trust Jesus. Her heart was overflowing with love and anticipation. She felt changed by being in the company of Jesus, even if it was only for a brief moment of time.

The faithful worshipers of God who were long since dead had truly left behind a legacy of worship, including worship by dancing. Abia felt a generational tug in the core of her being that seemed to confirm the growing desire she had to dance once again. When Jesus had spoken those two words to her, "My dancer," she felt He had reached into her and placed destiny and purpose back into her heart.

Praise and worship rose within Abia's heart. Gratitude flooded her soul. Oh, how she longed for the day when her withered leg would be restored and she could physically worship Him in the dance!

Her mind had been a container that had stored away all the dance moves she wished her body could do. It held so many dance moves that it would indeed take two new legs and two new hips to perform them all! Abia's heart held His promise like a treasure in safekeeping. She could not explain why and where her faith was coming from. Yet she knew Jesus would make a way for her to dance once again. Of this, she was certain.

There was certainly a lot more of her story to come. Abia's eagerness to tell it was equally met by that of her mother, who anxiously want to hear once again about how Jesus had healed her daughter. It was not until Yaron appeared at the door to investigate the location of his daughter and wife that Hannah realized the darkness of the night that had surrounded them.

"It is late and tomorrow there is much work left to do, and we will need our sleep. Soon there will be another opportunity to finish your story. I know the ending, but never grow tired of hearing it!" Hannah said as they made their way to their beds.

CHAPTER II

Royal Deceptions

While many were asleep in their warm beds at night, others, during the cover of night, planned evil and destruction for some of the citizens of Jerusalem. As the wickedness continued, it spilled over into the light of day.

Warnings to be cautious were given daily, as if the strong Roman presence at every corner was not enough of a reminder. No one was safe from the Romans' watchful eyes. Tolerance for Jewish people was draining away. The Romans had no appreciation of God or His ways, which made it a time of great moral decline and degradation. The deterioration did not originate with the current government, but it had not lessened with time.

The evil hand of injustice had made its ugly mark on everything it touched. Religious leaders were being corrupted by bribes paid by some Roman government officials to ward off Jewish skirmishes over the new religious leader named Jesus. Temple money changers were cheating the people who made daily sacrifices by padding the weights to make the items they purchased for sacrifice more expensive. Unfortunately, some of the special teachers of the Torah became greedy. Knowing how much they were admired by their fellow Jews, they took advantage of the opportunity to collect from the Roman soldiers special favors or even money to laugh away the miracles that were occurring daily. Some were given Roman protection for any assistance offered to them to damage the reputations of John the Baptist or Jesus of Nazareth.

It was learned that Herod Antipas and his wife Herodias were behind much of the deception. Some of the royal palace kitchen slaves came daily for their supply of fresh fruits and vegetables sold in marketplace. The wives of shopkeepers where known to engage the cooks and market slaves in conversations with the hope of finding some juicy tidbit of gossip to share with the other wives. The palace walls were thick, but information about the goings on behind the walls of the royal couple found its way to the marketplace quiet easily. Herod Antipas and Herodias were often the objects of much attention.

While some of the men scolded their wives for listening to gossip, they listened to the rumors nonetheless. When the men gathered together after the morning rush of customers, they enjoyed steaming hot cups of black tea. Their conversations of daily political and social events often included their piece of the gossip puzzle, which came from their wives.

Herod desired to be made king of the region, not merely tetrarch, and Herodias, who possessed even greater ambition than her husband, wanted to be made queen. To achieve their goals, they needed the Roman council to come to full understanding of and agreement with Herod's great leadership capabilities. For this to occur, a false impression must be made. The uprisings of the past had created much doubt in the mind of the Roman Emperor about Antipas' ability to rule as governor and even more about his ability to function as king of the Jews.

Herodias aimed to have her ambitions fulfilled and was determined to let nothing stand in her way. She set out to clean up Antipas' mistakes made by his laziness, negligence, and weak leadership skills over the Jewish people. Even a man considered by many as a prophet would not deter Herodias from her goals. When he spoke out publicly against them, John the Baptist was a threat to the magical delusions she was trying to paint for Roman government.

Rumor had it that Herod Antipas was somewhat afraid of John and his growing popularity. At best he was superstitious of John, knowing him to be a righteous and holy man. Antipas was perplexed as to what to do with John since he had come to enjoy listening to him from time to time. He found John to be quick-witted and challenging, both qualities of which the palace household sadly lacked.

Yaron and his friends laughed and elbowed each other when they spoke of Herod Antipas and Herodias' relationship. If the truth were known, they would have said that Herod Antipas was afraid of his Herodias, his newest wife. She was already nagging him to go to Rome and demand to be given the official title of king from her brother, Herod Agrippa. She had social and political control over her husband and was no doubt using her womanly wiles when necessary to gain much more. So to appease his wife, he arrested John, bound him, and put him into prison. The older men agreed this may have been a temporary fix to silence her.

Yaron also heard rumors at the street market that Herodias would go to great lengths to get revenge against John. Keeping her husband's name spotless was becoming a full-time job and one Herodias did not want to have for much longer. If Antipas did not give her the title she so desperately sought, she would marry again to obtain it, no matter how badly John the Baptist frowned upon doing so. Her lust for a title ignited an obsessive hatred toward John. She had already locked him away in prison, but putting him into prison had not stopped his message from continuing. And John now had a collaborator and superior by the name of Jesus working to spread the same message.

As a warning to others to think twice before publicly criticizing the royal family, Herodias felt John the Baptist needed to be silenced by whatever means necessary. Even if she had to have him murdered, he had to be stopped. Waiting patiently for a convenient or opportune time, this spider was busy building her web of destruction.

The marketplace buzzed with the newest information from palace servants, who described raised voices and temper tantrums when Herodias did not have her way. It was rumored that Herod had a wandering eye and would tolerate Herodias' outbursts for only so long. Some heard Herod had been seeking the attention of Salome, Herodias' young daughter and his niece. She would serve just as well as her mother to satisfy his ambitious political and social goals. Of this, Herodias would have no part.

Herodias knew her position was always precarious and something that was not to be taken for granted. By being married to Herod Antipas, she enjoyed a position of great wealth and social standing, but she was a woman in a man's world. It was a male-driven society led by self-indulgent men. She knew Herod Antipas may have regretted their marriage, especially when his former father-in-law was talking of waging war against him. It would be prudent to remember the rules of this game and that patience was her greatest weapon. Her own ambitions of title and position had to take a back seat to Herod Antipas' goals, at least until a better plan was devised. Until then, she remained mindful of the fact that her life was good and rich. To keep it, she knew she had to do whatever it took to remain on Herod's good side. Her temper tantrums had to turn quickly into sly and wily pouts to hastily apprehend the affection and attention of Herod once again.

The old men pondered how far Herodias would go to increase her control. Would she go as far as using her daughter, Salome, as a pawn? By using her daughter, would she be assured of a greater position than she now possessed? The palace servants and slaves could only shake their baffled heads as they contemplated Herodias' logic.

CHAPTER 12

The Dancing Healer

With only a few days to complete the sewing project before the long-awaited birthday celebration was to occur, everyone was feeling the push to complete their particular assignments. Time inside the Ben-David household seemed to be at a standstill with the added pressure to begin final preparations of the fabrics that were to be delivered soon. It was sometimes easy to forget the outside world when one worked inside so much.

While they worked, the strain was having its effect on them all. Everyone was growing weary and needed to hear some good news to focus on while they worked. Hannah suggested to Abia that perhaps she could tell again about the time when Jesus healed her.

So Abia continued her story by telling of the events of almost a year ago after Samuel had taken her to see Jesus and she had heard Him call her His dancer.

It was at the time when Jesus had heard that John had been put in prison and He departed to Galilee. Jesus left Nazareth and moved to Capernaum, which was by the sea. He gathered together 12 men whom He called disciples and taught them daily about the Kingdom of God. They traveled all over Galilee with Jesus and witnessed great miracles and healings. Many people began to follow Jesus, desperately seeking their healing, and Jesus taught the disciples how to heal people as well.

Reports of Jesus healing people spread like wildfire. People had witnessed Jesus healing all kinds of sicknesses and diseases. It was said He could heal people who were afflicted with demon-possession, epilepsy, and paralysis.

Abia had heard that Jesus was said to be heading to Jerusalem. She was reminded of the time a few months prior when Samuel took her to see Jesus at the insistence of her friend Mary. "My dancer" He had called her, awakening in her the hope that He would heal her so she could once again dance. *Could today be the day He will heal me?* Abia wondered. She had to know. With great excitement and trepidation, she asked Yaron to take her to Jesus.

The cart was loaded for the trip to Jerusalem. Great multitudes of people were following Jesus, and Abia and her family were among them. Samuel lifted her onto a blanket in the back of the cart, and off they went.

Abia's heart beat faster as each mile took them closer to Jesus. "Please, God, heal me so I can worship You with my whole body and soul," she whispered repeatedly.

So many people lined the dirt road, and Abia started to wonder if Jesus would ever be able to see her. Along the way, she saw many wounded and hurting people. Some, like her, were being carried by whatever means available. There were old and young, rich and poor, men and women, Jews and Gentiles, believers and unbelievers alike—all wanting and waiting for Jesus to come near.

Yaron decided to pull the cart near the water's edge to rest and be refreshed by the wind that swept across the water. "This will be a good place to wait," he said. Hannah and Judith were busy preparing the next meal. It was the time of year when the daylight heat would melt quickly when night approached, and a fire would also be needed.

A blanket for Abia was spread near the fire. Her neck began to ache from the constant movement back and forth as she watched for any signs of Jesus' approach. The heat of the day and the long trip had finally caught up with her, and she found herself lying back onto the blanket for some much needed rest. Even her dreams were filled with thoughts of healing.

A struggle raged within Abia as to whether she would be healed or not. In her dream, she saw once again the faces of the hurting multitudes they had met along their way. One in particular stood out among the rest. He was an old man, paralyzed from the waist down, and he had no one to help him. With only his arms to walk with, he was dragging his emaciated legs down the uneven road. Abia wondered, *Who am I to think God would allow me to be healed when others need it so much more?*

An evil voice mocked her as she prayed in her dream for the ability to walk once again. "You aren't good enough. He will never be able to find you. He doesn't remember you and won't bother with you. Your heart is filled with anger and bitterness. What possible use could you be to Him?" the menacing voice screeched.

"No, no, no," she responded, shaking her head back and forth, "He will find me. He will heal me."

Suddenly, Abia awoke from her dream. The sun was beginning to set as darkness silently slid over the land just as it had filled her head in the dream. Her mind was filled with doubt and unbelief once again. Dark shadows of pain and resentment slowly rose to the surface of her heart and spilled into her thoughts.

As bitter tears made tracks down Abia's face, she remembered the physical pain, but worse was the pain to her heart. Most of her childhood friends had rejected her when they realized she was no longer able to run and play. As she grew older, the young girls sang a song with poisonous lyrics inspired by religious, superstitious parents: "Abia is cursed by hidden sin, and God's punishment is firm. She will never marry, nor a mother will she ever be."

When Abia finally came out from the safety of her house and walked with the assistance of the wooden crutch, she met more heartache. The young men her age gazed upon her long enough to have their curiosity satisfied. Then quickly they averted their eyes in fear that she might misinterpret their stares of pity for attraction.

The silent nod beneath her hooded veil confirmed that their opinion of her matched the one she had of herself. Abia was broken, a useless oddity, and was doomed to spend the rest of her life watching life pass by, but not as a contributor.

Abia's body stored the physical pain and evidence of the incident, but her mind became the storage bin of buried emotional trauma and pain too savage to comprehend. She came to believe the messages from the stares of the young men and the poisonous ideas behind the wicked songs that were sung by the girls. The children confirmed her insignificance and the low value she held for herself. Through the years, she shook hands and made friends with these beliefs. It was a way to cope with the pain; besides, they felt so true.

When Jesus referred to Abia as "His dancer," her heart jumped alive with hope, but His declaration caused her to discover her true mindset and belief structures. *My dancer* challenged her to confront her beliefs and to make assessments between facts and truth. Do I really believe He could heal me? *Do I really believe He wants to heal me? Do I have the courage to believe either or both?*

A crippled piece of humanity with no worth did not add up to the prophetic title of "His dancer" that He had proclaimed when she last saw Him. Did she dare give birth to hope when all other attempts lay stillborn within her? No longer did she possess anything that could awaken faith on its own. Her truth had won out. The conflict was over. She had decided long ago to resign herself to the evidence that was clearly before her: she was lame and would never dance again. Hope saw her through many trials, but to remain loyal to such hope was dishonest. Facts are facts, and in that reality she needed to dwell.

Smug with all the answers to life's most complicated questions, Abia laid her back onto the blanket made warm by the crackling fire. Yet she could not shake her questions. *Why do tears of sadness and regret fill my ears?* she wondered.

With a jolt, Abia sat straight up. She felt a familiar presence nearby and heard Him whistle the joyful, recognizable tune. All of her newly-formed piety regarding life's injustices and the correct, mature way to handle them was thrown away as she began to shout at the top of her voice, "Papa! Momma! Samuel! Judith! Jesus is near! Jesus is near!"

Jesus' laugh filled the darkness and chased away all gloom. The firelight danced on His face as He stepped out of His boat at the water's edge. Abia watched with excitement as He surveyed the crowds of people and eagerly looked at each person.

"Abia, I've been looking for you," He said, turning in her direction. She knew in that moment, if she would never walk normally again or was asked to give up her dream of dancing, it would still be well with her soul because Jesus had called her by name. He had searched for her and found her.

"Yes, Lord, it is I, Abia," she said meekly as she peered over the veil that hid her face. She could not keep her eyes from His. The love and acceptance she saw in His eyes reflected an identity for her that was vastly different than the one she had for herself. She sensed that the ever-increasing evidences of facts she presumed to be true about herself could be exchanged for His truth—if she dared to believe.

"I think you owe Me a dance," He said, offering her His hand.

Abia knew that taking His hand required a measure of faith. She shyly lifted her hand to Him, waiting for the familiar tug she had grown accustomed to when someone offered her a hand to move or assist her in some way. It did not come. Suddenly, she realized that it was up to her to stand. She had a choice. When she looked deeply into His eyes, she knew she could do anything with His help. Nothing seemed impossible, not even for a deformed hip and lame leg that had not stood unassisted for 12 years.

As Abia started to move her legs, they were filled with warmth. It penetrated deep into her bones. Hotter than the homemade ointments that once burned her hip and leg, this warmth left no marks, but ignited a response. Looking about her for the wooden crutch, Abia soon realized it would never be needed again. She stood, and as she did, Jesus took her by both hands and whirled her around and around in a circle dance of joy.

Tears of thankfulness filled His eyes as He looked Heavenward. Then He shouted for all to hear, "My dancer!"

Jumping, twirling, and praising Jesus with each and every turn, Abia moved in delight. Her eyes were filled with tears of happiness and an overwhelming sense of gratitude. She danced with her Papa and Momma, with Samuel, and with Judith. Laughter and joy filled their hearts, and in humility they all landed on the ground to worship Jesus. Abia wasn't sure how long they were there, but when she eventually looked up, He was gone.

People from all around came to see for themselves what Jesus had done for Abia. Some cried with joy and praised God. Others stood some distance away with their curiosity satisfied, lief still filled their minds. Suddenly, from some distance could hear the echo of excited cries from people when Jesus came near to them as they declared, "I can walk!" "I can see!" "I can hear!" "I'm healed!" Joining the earthly chorus and acknowledging to all, Abia shouted, "I can dance!"

Abia's heart cup ran over with praise and thanksgiving each and every time she stood up and walked. Friends and family from near and far came to witness for themselves the miracle they had heard about. As the days passed, people's curiosity seemed to wane, but her faith increased. Jesus had saved from her from herself. The truth He spoke of surpassed the evidence of facts she had held to be true in her mind. She wondered, *Could it be that my reality prevented me from accepting His truth, and when I made the decision to accept His truth for mine, I was healed?*

Physically she was healed, but she was also healed emotionally. She had come to this realization: *How can I answer the prophetic call to dance while holding onto the thoughts that crippled me?*

Abia determined that forever she would bless the name of Jesus. His name would always remind her of the goodness of God. Never would she forget the benefits of having God as their Father and the privilege of being called His people. He who forgives all iniquities and heals all diseases shall forever be praised. He who had redeemed her life from destruction and crowned her with loving kindness and tender mercies would be honored for all time. Abia knew she could love Him because He had first loved her. "Bless the Lord, O my soul, all that is within me," she sang. King David's words had never been so true to her. *Praise the Lord!*

A year had passed from the monumental day when Jesus healed Abia along the shores of the Sea of Galilee. In many ways, her life was much the same as it had always been, filled with hard work and never ending chores, but that was not entirely true. Each day of her life was now a dance of its own. Every time she moved her feet and legs to the rhythmic beat of everyday life, she saw it as a form of worship, and she excitedly danced to every song.

Abia's season of mourning had passed, and the new season to dance had begun. She celebrated every movement of the dance, including the ability to painlessly sit, stand, kneel, bend, stretch, reach, kick, step, turn, jump, skip, run, twist, and spin in a circle. No longer needed, the wooden crutch served only as a reminder of Jesus' touch that had healed her and the grace He had extended toward her.

Much had happened in a short amount of time. Everything seemed to be changing, and nothing seemed to stay as it was. Solomon's own words described the season of time that was upon Abia and her family. He said, there is *an appointed time for everything. And there is a time for every event under heaven.*

In the room that once felt like her prison, Abia continued to sew, but with renewed vitality, energy, and a zest for life. With the deadline fast approaching, the Ben-David family diligently worked to complete the sewing order issued from Herod's palace for his birthday celebrations.

CHAPTER 13

A Change of Plans

The mounting tension and violence in the streets of Jerusalem made Yaron especially hesitant to hand deliver the dining cushions, table covers, towels, and napkins to the palace as he had promised Akil, the head social planner in the palace of Herod. Over and over again, Yaron spoke of his regret for giving his assurance to Akil when all the sewing was completed.

Yet, Yaron was a man of integrity, and what he promised he would personally see through until its completion. He was a man of his word, and his sense of duty and responsibility was strong.

Yaron muttered a quick prayer to thank God for his conscientious and hard-working family. Not only did the job get finished on schedule, there was a little time to spare. This would permit them to make the delivery and get back before the sun cast shadows on people's faces and darkness covered friend and foe alike. Comforted by his plan, he and Samuel placed each hand-stitched item carefully on the cart.

Yaron had promised Abia, Judith, and Hannah they could ride with him and Samuel while they made the delivery as a reward for the hard work. Hannah decided against going in favor of resting at home from the two weeks of long, hard work.

The height of the defensive walls and the conspicuous guards stationed all about the palace's rim left a lasting impression that uninvited visitors would not be welcomed. This was a chance of a lifetime, and everyone eagerly looked forward to catching a glimpse of the mysteries behind the palace walls. And Hannah looked forward to hearing about it when they returned.

Yaron's excited expressions soon turned to serious ones as he explained the procedure to enter the palace. Armed with written permission given by Akil, they would transport the goods into the palace gates from the east side. Akil had explained how, once they were inside, he would have a slave boy ready to lead them to the kitchen's side entrance. The boy would briefly leave them at the kitchen entrance while he retrieved final written authorization from within the palace, allowing entry into the great banqueting hall, where they would hand deliver the sewn items to Akil himself. With the meeting planned, all that was left to do was to pack, and their journey could begin.

Exhilaration soon overtook all previous fatigue as the mule-pulled cart was finally loaded with the beautiful handcrafted wares and was made ready to go. Samuel would ride on the seat as Judith, Papa, and Abia planned to walk behind the cart, standing guard on all three sides. Yaron wanted to see for himself that the cart remained steady and able to ward off any potential problems with the fabrics as they traveled the bumpy road to the palace.

Samuel looked back at his father, who had checked and re-checked the goods that were placed inside something that looked much like a giant pillowcase that lay low on the flat part of the small cart. The fabric lining would keep dirt away from the pristine white materials that were used, so the immaculately laundered linens were safely tucked inside. Samuel tried to wait patiently for the signal to begin and prayed the beast that carried the cart could do the same.

With a nod, the small caravan moved forward until Yaron gave Samuel a shout to stop the proceedings immediately only a few yards from its origins. With instructions to stay put, they heard him mumbling under his breath something about leaving some important documents behind and something else no one could understand.

Yaron quickly ran back into the house to ask Hannah one more time if she indeed preferred staying at home to rest rather than going with the family to see the palace.

"Go!" Hannah said. "I will be fine and am looking forward to a long-needed nap. You, my husband, Yaron Ben-David, have truly worked my fingers to the bones!" she remarked waving her ten digits high in the air.

Seeing her framed in the doorway, he laughed and was reminded once again of the goodness of God for having blessed him with such a fine and loyal wife.

"Have you seen the important documents that we will need to enter the palace gates?" He inquired of his wife as he frantically surveyed the rooms once more.

Very gently she placed her hand upon Yaron's breast, and as she did, the documents' safe hiding place was rediscovered.

"You are a good wife, my Hannah!" he said as he quickly made his way to the door.

Hurriedly, he reached for the mezuzah which hung on the doorpost and kissed the fingers that touched it. God indeed was always present in their lives. How Yaron loved and respected God and His laws and was reminded once again of his duty to fulfill them.

Carelessly, Yaron's left foot caught the solid casing on the side of the door, causing him to tumble to the ground instead of onto the fully loaded cart. Dazed from fatigue and from the sudden impact of the fall, Yaron rolled up his pant leg to reveal his worst fear. A purplish-blue color was already making its way to his skin from around the knee cap. Hannah, Samuel, Judith, and Abia arrived at the same time and quickly saw what he had already seen. Samuel and Hannah lifted Yaron from the ground and guided him back into the house, pausing only long enough to once again touch the mezuzah.

Seated on his bed, Hannah quickly took a wet towel and wrapped his knee. Through pain-filled eyes, he confirmed everyone's suspicions: the swollen knee made the decision for him. Yaron had no other choice but to send the rest of his family on without him. Hannah's quiet nap now a dream of the past, she quickly set about making things comfortable for her husband. The training she had received when Abia was five years old once again served her family well.

Samuel took from Yaron the parchment giving permission to enter the royal gates. Samuel, Judith, and Abia stood silently while the final directions were made, despite waves of pain that radiated from Yaron's knee. Abia knew full well the pain he was suffering and forced herself to listen to him as he hurriedly prepared them for the journey.

"Follow Akil's instructions precisely. Keep the fabrics clean and give them to no one except Akil. Do not indulge yourself in idle curiosity. Take care of your sisters, Samuel. Girls, stay with Samuel and do not leave his side. You will complete the job, and when you return home, you will tell me and Momma of your wonderful adventures," Yaron finished with a weakened smile. The pain in his knee was throbbing with intensity that caused him to lean back upon his bed exhausted.

Hannah nodded to them her approval and silently said a quick prayer for Yaron's knee and her children's safety as they made their way to the cart and on to King Herod Antipas' palace.

CHAPTER 14

Festive Illusions

The palace guards received the letter of entrance from the royal social planner, Akil, without hesitation. They were to report directly to him, and to him were they to give up their precious parcels. A palace slave led them past the royal gardens and glimmering pools to the chaos of the kitchen area near the great banqueting hall. More than once, Samuel had to scold Judith and Abia for slowing down their pace to gaze at the marvelous sights only wondered about until now. Samuel carried the biggest bulk of the merchandise, while Judith and Abia struggled with the rest.

At last the palace servant silently directed the three to Akil, the man totally responsible for the social event of the year. With a quick introduction, the palace servant bowed swiftly away from the menacing man, his mission accomplished.

The dark, demanding gaze of the imposing man frightened all of them, although Samuel would never have admitted it to his two younger sisters. With growing fascination, their eyes drank in the sights as they waited until Akil had finished discussing the final arrangements with the head table-dresser.

The immense banqueting hall was filled with low sitting tables, all angling outward, with the royal table at the apex. The elaborate decorations from the floor to the ceiling made the tables awaiting our coverings look completely out of place and undressed.

Akil's penetrating look assessed Samuel at once. "Where is your father?" his inquiry sounding more like a warning.

Samuel met the man eye to eye and explained how Papa suffered from an injury just before making the delivery.

Akil gave two quick claps, and his long, dark finger pointed to the table covers. Assistance came immediately to relieve Samuel and the girls of their cargo. A look of impatience, or maybe relief, crossed Akil's face as he assessed the royal blue tablecloths with matching brilliantly white overlays. He seemed somewhat relieved by the finished product. It was Papa's hope that their work would far surpass Akil's expectations, and from the look of appreciation that flashed across Akil's face, the goal was achieved.

Immediately the servants began to dress the tables. With more claps, Akil signaled the other servants to take the heavily padded, royal blue and white kneeling cushions especially designed for the long elegant dining tables. Two young slave girls shyly gathered from Abia and Judith the embroidered hand towels and napkins and placed them on serving tables discreetly hidden behind the royal ones. When the royal blue and white striped banner (one banner) bearing the initial "H" framed in gold was hung high upon the wall behind the guest of honor's table, it was the crowning touch.

As much as Samuel enjoyed seeing the works of their hands being displayed, the man Akil fascinated him more. Akil was a man who knew elegance, yet commanded respect as much as any military officer Samuel had ever seen. He seemed calm while under pressure, and others looked to him with respect—or was it fear? The servants surrounding Akil awaited his familiar bark of instructions or the loud beat from his hand claps that spoke a language they seemed to understand. Akil had every right to have leather straps beat their backs if his orders were not carried out implicitly the first time. With almost army-trained precision, the servants each attended to their assigned tasks.

Turning his dark face in Samuel's direction, Akil bowed from the waist. "Young Yaron Ben-David, please send my condolences to your father for his injury. Congratulate him for the fine artistry with which he and his family graced the palace of Herod on this special day until I can personally do so," he concluded with another bow and turned his attention to the affairs of the festivities.

Samuel, Judith, and Abia watched the brightly colored turban worn by Akil until it disappeared from sight. Papa would be thankful his instructions had been followed so completely and his prayers answered so perfectly. It was agreed Akil's words brought satisfaction and relief to them all.

Watching each item being placed in its designated spot, one could not help but remember its humble beginnings. The Ben-David family's meager home business housed the items, and from skilled fingers these beautiful creations were formed. It brought great pleasure knowing the items were appreciated and valued. All glory and honor was given to God for making it all possible.

They permitted themselves another look at the embroidered regal "H" that graced the center of the table where the most powerful citizens of Galilee would soon be gathered. It was good to know Akil valued the work even though he may not have appreciated the God-given talents needed to complete such a task. As Samuel contemplated the upcoming event, he believed others placed a different value on the items they made. The emblem was strategically placed as a reminder to all; the extravagance and excellent craftsmanship was meant as a compliment to its bene-factor and a means to extol the success of the influential governor. If the rumors were true, these items were designed to enhance the status of the sometimes insecure Herod Antipas, the governor who wanted to be made Herod Antipas the king.

Given what people were saying in the marketplace of late, this cel-ebration would meet with a variety of opinions, Samuel thought to himself, as he pondered the purpose of the celebration and the ru-mors that were stirred as a result from it. He imagined that the in-fluential guests invited to the celebration would indeed be amazed by the flaunting of Herod's wealth as he sought to prove his suffi-ciency to lead his kingdom. Some would indeed be impressed. For others, all the efforts in the world would not impress or convince them of Herod's leadership skills. If the gossip mill was correct, these opinions would not change, regardless of Herod's obvious display of success and wealth.

Some men had said that the military leaders judged Antipas as cunning as his father, Herod the Great, but they knew he lacked his father's gift of diplomacy. With rumors of a potential war with his first wife's father, some military officials had major concerns about his talent for war. Their reasons for being at the birthday party were for fact-finding purposes only, although Herod Anti-pas might be none the wiser.

The rumors also mentioned how some dignitaries had another agenda for attending the party. As they rubbed elbows with the richest people in the known world, they hoped to find business connections or new clients for export or import trade. The nag-ging and harassment of some extremely spoiled and bored wives would bring some men to the party, according to reports by some of the women who had overheard the rich women talking on more than one occasion. Others guests had no hidden agenda at all and wanted to come to the celebration because they never missed a royal party, no matter what, some scandalous gossipers reported.

Taking a final look at the table coverings and the other items sown by the Ben-David family, Samuel was once again truly amazed at their beauty. God had blessed their family with talent, and they had been taught to give credit where credit was due. Pondering whether they should be complimented by the honored place the needlework occupied or be wary that it was to be used as a prop in a well-rehearsed and devious play, he knew no one could say with any degree of accuracy at this time. Something told him the latter would be more true.

CHAPTER 15

Lost in Beauty

Samuel's elbow nudged Judith and Abia to indicate it was time to go back home. Jahi, a fragile, fearful, young slave, perhaps 18 years old, was assigned the task of quickly escorting them from the banqueting hall. He led them in a different direction from the way they had come, which afforded them an opportunity to see another section of the palace which they might never be allowed to see again. Along the way, Abia felt thankful for the headpiece that covered and protected her inquisitive, wide eyes.

The grand banquet hall was filled with an enormous flurry of activity, exotic smells, and lavish preparation. They observed how wildly chaotic everything looked while everyone darted to and fro. Judith and Abia had long speculated from the safety of their shared bedroom what was behind the walls of the palace and what sights were held there. This celebration must indeed be an extremely special occasion to warrant such effort and expense.

"Be gone!" Akil's voice yelled to Jahi, warning him they had lingered perhaps a little longer than was necessary. Jahi was visibly shaken by his master's voice and made greater effort to remove them from the room.

With so much preparation still to be attended to and every one of Herodias' details to be obeyed, Akil may have agreed with their unvoiced assessment of chaos. He had personally been assigned the overseeing of this highly important occasion, and he must once again demonstrate that his wisdom and knowledge of such pageantry was invaluable, despite his increasing age. His impeccable taste and his subtle flattery made Akil Herodias' favorite. She knew her countless number of demands and itemized lists would be carried out without excuse or hesitation. She also depended on Akil's discretion and his willingness to keep her little secrets. Was it chaotic? Yes, by appearances only. This birthday was planned with as much strategy and precision as any battle of the esteemed Roman military quests.

Giant marble columns stood as guards along the promenade between the banqueting hall and the royal throne room. The mousy servant, Jahi, decided on a short cut from the promenade to the royal gardens. It was his hope to be rid of them as quickly as possible and escape from the dark, all-seeing eyes of Akil. Samuel matched the servant's steps leaving Judith and Abia some distance behind. So determined to leave the palace and to obey Akil, the two seemed to have forgotten the two girls as their long legs pushed forward.

Jahi made a sudden quick turn into a small, hidden hallway leading directly into the gardens. It took a few moments for Judith and Abia to realize Samuel and Jahi were nowhere to be found. The beautiful billowing fabric cascading from each side of the high arches caught their attention. It was then that Judith tripped and hit her head on the hard surface of the beautiful mosaic floor.

Suddenly, the trumpeters' short blasts announced to all that the festivities were about to begin. Judith's cries of pain were blocked by the sound of the trumpets. Like two birds in a proverbial trap, Judith and Abia were unable to escape. The columns of stone to their backs and a veil of beautifully sheer cloth to their front became their cage. Wildly, Abia's eyes tried to scope the massive hallways and giant rooms for the familiar outline of her brother, and the trembling frame of Jahi.

All hope slowly drained from Abia as realization dawned—the two were nowhere to be found. Judith was in shock from either the trauma to her head or from fear, making it impossible to run. In a split second, Abia decided to remain still for the time being. The guests were beginning to spill into the hallway blocking the route. To stay put seemed the safest course of action, and it would prevent unwanted attention.

An eternity of time seemed to pass before their breath could slowly return to normal and be exhaled behind the safety of the beautiful silk enclosure. Judith's eyes were filled with pain and regret as she stared helplessly at Abia, begging for forgiveness. With a quick wink and a benevolent smile of understanding, Abia whispered sisterly reassurance. Since Abia's healing, she had discovered she was more adventurous than Judith by nature. As fear gave way to curiosity, Abia quickly realized they had been given choice seats for viewing the whole birthday celebration.

Pain and panic kept Judith's eyes closed, preventing her from appreciating their circumstances. Abia's emotions were a strange mix of excitement and dread. The trumpets and the guards reminded her of the precarious position they found themselves in. Although it was an incredible vantage point from which to see all the festivities, the position could not be taken for granted. If discovered, Heaven only knew what would become of them or their family.

Abia's mind meandered from apprehension to fear to excitement and back again. Sometimes the soft groans of pain from Judith sounded like pounding drums to her panic-stricken ears, assuring her their discovery was imminent. As she looked into her sister's eyes, Abia saw more pain than her mouth had expressed. Compassion gripped her as she helped her to lie on the cool marble floor and gathered her as close as possible. "Help, hide, heal, and protect us, God," became their whispered, corporate prayer. Soon His peace flooded their hearts, and they gained confidence from the knowledge that their prayers had indeed been heard. They were safe, at least for the time being.

Judith found her voice as the cool marble added some relief to her headache. "I'm so sorry, Abia. It is not like me to be so clumsy and awkward, but my eyes were drawn upward enthralled by the fabrics and colors," she said with embarrassment reddening her cheeks. Momma and Papa had said of Judith that her face was always turned Heavenward, as if she were expecting a holy kiss. Abia was sure their parents would not be at all surprised when they heard of this mishap and that the cause was from the tilt of Judith's head.

Their Momma had trained and modeled for the two of them how to pray, to worship God in everything they did, to love His Word, and to live lives with gratitude. Dancing had once again become Abia's favorite expression of worship and praise to God. She had discovered since being healed that she was not overtly athletic, but had a certain grace and agility inherited from a long lineage of dancers among their people. They heard the age-old stories of Miriam and King David from childhood. Dancing in the Ben-David family was as natural as prayer; in fact, they had been taught they were one and the same. Abia's heart used to ache when those old stories were told, fearing she would never be able to join in the dance herself. God knew the desire of her heart and had given back to her what she had longed for.

One by one, the long processional of lords, military command-ers, political dignitaries, and other leading men of the region was announced to Herod Antipas and his wife, who were assembled in the great throne room. Herod Antipas and Herodias were pre-tentiously seated on two incredibly beautiful regal thrones. The series of marble steps leading to the royal thrones gave the height and appearance of superiority due a king and his queen. From the steps, servants approached and delivered with a bow the lavish birthday gifts from all of the invited guests, starting with the most influential and ending with the least. As each gift offering was made, the dignitary was escorted into the main banqueting hall a short distance away from the great throne room by impressively dressed palace guards and servants. There they were immediately served wine and other delicacies as they waited for the royal cou-ple to join them.

The ornate banqueting room was filled with the repeated gold, silver, white, purple, and royal blue color theme Herodias had insisted upon. Wine was already flowing freely by the time the final guests were seated along the low-lying tables. Herod and Herodias had not yet joined their guests, but were admiring the lavish gifts that had been bestowed upon them.

Everything from jeweled rings to magnificent horses had been given, with the intention of impressing the governor as well as the other guests. For some, their gifts were no sacrifice at all. They used their gifts with intimidation in mind to create insecurity in Herod Antipas. Those gifts were used to show the immensity of the givers' own empires and prove how worthy they would be to rule Herod's lands as well. For others, their gifts were indeed a sacrifice, but nevertheless used as tools to flatter Herod Antipas with the hope of personal gain.

In the banqueting hall every servant had been given strict instructions to keep every cup filled with wine and every plate filled with deliciously prepared foods. Self-indulgence and over-indulgence were the order of the day.

With great trumpet blasts the royal hostess and her husband entered the great banqueting hall and viewed their guests with great satisfaction. The night seemed to hold for the royal couple separate, private, and secret pleasures.

Herodias stood proudly among the gathered diplomats in the most exquisite red gown Abia had ever seen. In grandiose fashion she carefully delivered her well-rehearsed speech. She thanked the esteemed guests and complimented them for their loyalty and allegiance to her husband, Herod. It sounded as smooth and as sweet as the incredible desserts they were soon to enjoy from the royal kitchens. After the applause subsided, Herodias then turned her attention to her husband and reassured him much effort had been made to celebrate his birth, and no one was more deserving. This brought forth yet another round of applause from all over the great hall. With a flamboyant sweep of her bare arm, she ended her address by promising Herod Antipas and his esteemed guests greater surprises yet to come.

CHAPTER 16

Brotherly Love

Samuel and Jahi walked as swiftly as possible, all the while trying not to be noticed by the palace guards. Although they had permission to be there, Akil had ordered them out quite awhile ago. Fear and worry made them look guilty. When two Roman soldiers quickly turned in their direction, they panicked and began looking for a place to hide. Jahi's dark apprehensive stares validated Samuel's assessment. As if their fears increased simultaneously, they both took action. Hiding behind one of the huge mosaic flowerpots that surrounded the royal gardens, anxiety and distress sank even more deeply into the pit of Samuel's stomach. As if the soldiers had more pressing issues to attend to than the four of them, they swiftly turned in another direction.

As Samuel and Jahi breathed a sigh of relief, they turned their attention behind them to check on Abia and Judith, when fear gripped them like a vise. They were safe from the soldiers, but where were Samuel's sisters?

All the blood seemed to drain from both of them at the same time upon discovering the girls had not kept pace with them and were lost from their view. Without a word, both young men jumped to their feet. Just as they turned to retrace their steps, the same two Roman soldiers hastily marched toward them once again. Hiding behind a large statue of some Roman goddess, they hoped it would provide enough protection from the probing eyes of the officers assigned to guarding the massive halls within the palace.

They gave another sigh of relief as the soldiers marched past them, only to see the soldiers meet with the other soldiers at the end of the hall. The soldiers were animated with great excitement. In Samuel's already terrified mind, he imagined this could only mean trouble for them or his sisters. With a quivering voice, Jahi, the servant boy, told Samuel he must follow him out of the palace and let the girls take care of themselves.

Samuel's thoughts were bombarded with concern and dread for Abia and Judith. He knew the heavy responsibility of their safety was his as the eldest and only son in the family. He had known this only too well. It was as if history was repeating itself. He had failed to keep Abia safe many years ago, and it was happening again. Fear of the palace guards and fear for his sisters' welfare split his heart in two.

As if sensing Samuel's dilemma, Jahi conveyed a plan to bring Samuel to safety outside the royal gate while he returned to search for the missing girls. With a promise to give him any news concerning his sisters, Samuel finally consented to leave the hiding place among the gardens and go to the outer palace gate.

Samuel despised himself for not taking better care of his sisters, and his heart grew heavy with worry. Not since his baptism had he felt so heavy-laden with guilt. In that moment of time, he felt completely helpless. Samuel lowered his head as he silently reached out to God in prayer, which was becoming as automatic as his next breath. From the shadows of the setting sun growing dim behind the palace walls, he began his continual intercession on behalf of his sisters to the all-knowing One.

CHAPTER 17

Cloak of Darkness

Pewter goblets were in the fists of each guest. They were constantly being refilled with royal wine, which gave its desired effect in record time. From behind Abia and Judith's hidden confine of beautiful silk, they could hear the voices of the richest people in the region. The conversations at first centered on kingdom and commonplace concerns: royal taxes, military triumphs, fast horses, hiring laborers, marketplace debates, monarch gossip, Passover preparations, cures for illnesses, building projects, Olympic games, and travel tales. These topics were among the many buzzing around the gigantic room.

Abia soon discovered, however, that the faster the wine consumption was, the freer the tongue became. Having been raised with a very strict moral code and with Yaron's intentional protection from the ways of the world, the sights and further conversations caught Abia totally off guard.

Yaron's tone and manner toward Hannah had always been filled with respect, with honor, and with a sweet tenderness that spoke only of love and devotion. Hannah's response to him was in like manner. Abia and Judith always enjoyed watching them together. What Judith and Abia were about to witness was so far removed from their personal experience that the mere thought of it did not have a place in their minds.

Wine, wine, and more wine flowed, coupled with the delectable foods that were now splattered on the beautiful table coverings the family had labored so long to make. As night settled outside the massive estate, an evil darkness was consuming the inside. With no regard to their surroundings or to the company they kept, these men and women of wealth and influence now acted no differently than ignorant peasants or animals from the streets.

All protocol and decorum were washed away and replaced with such acts of the flesh that Abia's stomach retched from viewing them. The voices of the people became so loud that there seemed to be a need to increase the volume in order to be heard. Streams of wine and morsels of food on the corners of the bearded faces of the men were being licked by the women as if they were dogs. The free movement of the men's hands on the bodies of the noble women and servants alike gave Abia's eyes no safe place to alight.

Abia's senses were being invaded by the worldly, the flesh, and sin in ways never before seen. In the cloak of such darkness, her innocence was being ripped from her, and there was nothing that could be done to keep it from happening. It was not safe to close her eyes because she had to be on high alert in fear of being discovered.

All the excitement and wonder first felt when they landed in such prime seating for the birthday celebration now died within Abia. Fear and dread gripped her from opposing sides, making her very much afraid now that they could be more than witnesses to such atrocities; if discovered, they might become part of them.

Abia's hearing and sight had become as keen as any prey with its predator so near. What she was hearing and seeing made her want to run and escape, but doing so would only make the two of them victims of such darkness.

Should they try to make a break for it and risk being discovered by the palace guards or stay where they were and risk being found by a drunken guest? One look at the terrible bruising that was already covering Judith's innocently sleeping face made the decision easy. It was impossible to tell if Judith's sleep was from a possible concussion or was a way to escape from the horrible sights that were now ever present. Either way, Judith could not be moved without causing a disturbance.

Only God could get them out of this, and in Him Abia would put her trust.

CHAPTER 18

Jahi, the Helpful

Jahi was true to his word to Samuel. He made his way back inside the banqueting hall. He knew he was risking life and limb to look for the two lost girls. He had seen from times past what happened to slaves who were not where they were supposed to be. He had also seen what happened to uninvited guests of the palace. Akil would have little or no patience with him or the Ben-David family, especially since they had been told to leave quite a while ago.

Jahi had not dared to share with Samuel that his greatest fear for the two girls was their being found by palace guards. What they might do to them was more than he wanted to explain to their brother. At least if Akil found the girls first, Jahi might be given an opportunity to explain. The guards listened to no one but their superiors. They would never give Jahi, a lowly slave, a chance to explain.

Silently Jahi entered the hall. His senses were immediately bombarded with the smell of sweet wine and rich food. The banquet was all going as planned by Akil and Queen Herodias. The servants were scurrying around making sure each guest had exactly what he or she desired. All of the slaves who were assigned to the servants had been warned and threatened with their lives if any complaints were registered. According to palace standards, the party was going very nicely. The guests seemed to be enjoying themselves with good food and loud conversation. In fact, they were talking to each other so loudly they paid no attention to him.

Just as he was making his way toward the giant columns arrayed with magnificently colored ribbons streaming from their tops, Jahi thought he saw something move within the coverings. If one had not been looking, the girls' hiding place would have been virtually impossible to see. He quickly caught sight of the two girls huddled within the cleverly designed cave. He was silently glad the girls had found such good covering and had kept their wits about them. They were safe enough for now, but he dared not risk disclosing their position by getting any closer.

Just then, a very drunken man was drawing closer and closer to the place where the girls were hiding. As quickly as possible, Jahi made his way toward the man, hoping some means of distraction would present itself. A fellow slave approached with a platter holding several vessels of wine. Jahi grabbed one of the goblets from the platter and offered it to the inebriated man. It was just the enticement the man needed. The intoxicated guest spun around greedily and took the goblet from Jahi's hand. As he did, he redirected the man's steps in the opposite direction and away from the girls.

Jahi bowed from the waist as if giving the man the wine was an honor and privilege. Feeling satisfied that the guest's needs were met, Jahi walked as quickly as possible from the banqueting hall.

He had to find Samuel with the news of his sisters' precarious position, but most importantly of their safety.

A sigh of relief was uttered by both Jahi and Samuel when they caught sight of each other. Jahi's report was punctuated with an audible prayer from Samuel, thanking God for his sisters' safety. Jahi quickly explained where the girls were located and how cleverly they were hidden. It was agreed that Samuel would go home to explain the whole incident to his parents. Jahi assured Samuel there was plenty of time if previous parties were any indication.

CHAPTER 19

Dance, the Weapon of Seduction

From the corner of her eye, Abia suddenly saw a mountainous military officer heading in their direction. His sandaled feet marched closer and closer. Just as suddenly, he spun back around and grabbed a new goblet of wine from the fist of Jahi, the servant boy who had been assigned to help them from the palace some time ago. Abia hoped Jahi saw their precarious predicament and would then tell Samuel of their location and inform him that at present they were quite safe.

The amusements began with a poetry reading packed with high praise for Rome and its loyal subjects. Gymnasts followed, causing the audience to gasp at the athletic physiques of the men and the raw strength they possessed. A storyteller gave a glorified summary of the lives of some guests, paying special tribute to the wealthiest and most powerful. Some of the guests appeared to become exasperated for not having their life stories summarized and others from hearing the amplification of the summaries. Just in time, the vagabonds came with comical relief. The vagabonds did animal tricks and feats of magic to lighten the mood.

Just as the last act exited, a huge gong sound was made. When the leather-bound mallet hit a giant cymbal hanging from a frame, it directed everyone's attention to the host's table. Herodias was about to make a speech.

"To my dear husband on the day of his birth and to all our esteemed guests, I ask you now to give attention to my next surprise. For your enjoyment and for your pleasure, I present this dance for your acceptance." With dramatic flair and staged precision, Herodias' arms swept outward directing everyone's gaze to the back of the great banqueting hall.

Drums began a slow, sensual beat. The giant torches flickered with each beat as seven female dancers all in a line slowly made their appearance. Each drum beat brought the barefoot dancers closer and closer to the front and center of the room. The dancers made an alluring pass around the room to the applause of the eager audience. It seemed as though the audience was expecting dancers and their applause showed they were well pleased.

Six dancers formed a circle around the single dancer. Each dancer had finger cymbals in each snake-like arm. Hip circles and hip twists followed each click of the cymbals as they traveled around the lone dancer in the middle of the circle. Occasionally, they moved away from the dancer in the center to give the appearance that the solo dancer was about to join the circle. It was soon discovered it was only a ploy to call attention to her and tease the audience. The birthday guests quickly shouted their disapproval when the single dancer stayed motionless at the hub.

All the dancers were dressed in exactly the same toga costumes and matching face veils, but each wore different vibrant colors. The silk no doubt came from the Orient and appeared to be extremely expensive. No element of this celebration was overlooked, and cost was of no consideration.

The first of the six dancers was dressed in a fiery orange dyed silk toga with a matching orange veil that barely concealed the beautiful face behind it. The toga was made from one long ribbon of very sheer orange silk. It looked as if she had been made to stand in the center of the ribbon while two people crisscrossed front and behind her until all that was left were two ends of the silk long enough to hold in her two hands. The dancer's body shape could easily be seen despite the numbers of times she was wrapped. Someone could easily grab one end of the fabric and with a strong tug spin her like a top until it fell in a heap at her naked feet, leaving a very exposed dancer.

When the fiery orange dancer left the circle she made her way to the middle of the floor drawing all the attention on her. The other five dancers lagged behind to provide a protective barrier for the distinct single dancer who was dressed in gold. The five dancers encircled the gold dancer, all the while moving seductively to the clanging of their finger cymbals as they stood in place. Almost in a posture of worship, the golden dancer knelt down with her head touching the floor and arms extended to each side of her head hiding most of her body and all of her face.

With sharp hip movements the orange dancer seductively danced toward one of Herod's distinguished male quests, an extremely wealthy trader of cinnamon, pepper, nutmeg, and cloves from India. He was on the outer edge of the table fully reclined four cushions down from Herod Antipas. Overfed and lightheaded from the wine, he was totally captivated by this new form of entertainment. The orange dancer was on the opposite side of the table as she swayed her body closer and closer toward him. Confident in her power of attraction over him she made accessible the orange veil that covered her face. To unveil a woman in public was considered disgraceful, but he was extremely curious to see the face behind the veil, and the wine he had consumed made him bold. Pressing her face close to his, she enticed him to rip the veil from her face. Just as he reached his trembling drunken hand out to follow her bidding, she dipped out of his reach with low shoulder shimmies. As he stood up bewildered, the audience exploded with laughter at his helplessness and her control over him.

His embarrassment and discomfort was rewarded when she approached him again to amorously stroke his face as if to beg his forgiveness. Tilting her head, she leaned her face tantalizingly close to his once again. This time she allowed him to forcefully remove the veil uncovering an exotically beautiful woman. While his sweaty hand held the orange veil, she spun away from him and danced in a wide circle for all to see and inspect her beauty.

Gradually, she made her way back to the man, who was excited to have the attention of such loveliness. The man became the center of interest once again as he yanked the orange ribbon belt of her toga she offered up to him. With the crowd's approval, he pulled the belt, forcing the dancer toward him, and as he did, she jumped into his arms and became his for the evening.

The audience exploded with passionate applause as their attention was once again focused on the circle of dancers with the golden dancer in the center. A glistening, sapphire blue dancer took her leave from the others in the circle. The music alternated from a slow pulsating beat to a hurried fervor and back again as the sapphire blue dancer took the orange dancer's place front and center of Herod Antipas' table.

With fluid movement of hips and hands the blue dancer began to pay close attention to another one of Herod's esteemed guests, this time a military leader. Following the pattern of the orange dancer, she danced her way toward him and offered him the opportunity to rip the blue veil from her face. Without delay he did as was expected, and once again the blue dancer slid her head to the right, and he just missed his attempt to unveil her. The audience went wild with their applause as his face reddened from the heat of being outwitted by a woman. As she completed her tease, he reached once again, determined he would not make the same mistake again. The man snatched the sapphire blue veil from her face and reached for the toga ribbon belt at the same time. As he pulled her closer, the audience just barely got a glimpse of her stunning beauty as he took her in his arms, and she was his for the evening.

Next the dark emerald green dancer replaced the shimmering blue dancer, which left three remaining dancers to protect the golden dancer in the center of the room. When the emerald green dancer found her partner and jumped into his arms, the cherry-red-colored dancer took her place, leaving two dancers to the protect the golden one. When the cherry red dancer found her partner and jumped into his arms, the deep purple dancer took her place. This left the shimmering silver dancer to follow.

As the shimmering silver dancer jumped into her partner's arms, everyone became silent. Even the drums stopped their feverish beat. The audience's eyes were drawn to the one who had not moved from the center of the room.

Dressed completely in a magnificent golden toga with a matching golden silky veil to cover her identity, the golden-colored dancer stayed motionless until a single drum beat was struck. The music became smooth and seductive. With all eyes upon her, the still-veiled gold dancer slowly stood from her prostrate position.

With exaggerated hip twists and shoulders that shimmied to the rhythmic thump of the drums, she made her way toward the honored guest's table. As she approached Herod Antipas, the music's rhythm cycled from a slow pounding to a fevered pitch while her hips pursued the beat.

Just as the dance reached its most suspenseful moment, the mysterious female offered Herod Antipas the end of the golden silky ribbon belt of her toga instead of the face veil, like the other dancers had done.

With each of Herod's attempts to grasp hold of the golden ribbon she spun playfully around and around just in time to keep him from successfully grabbing the end of the fabric. Again and again she offered him the end of the silk, and each time she again avoided his grasp. His anticipation grew as well as the audience's. He expected the best was saved for last. Glowing with pride, he would be the envy of all when he would be given the golden beauty for himself. He would be the talk of all of Rome and Galilee if the honor to unveil her could be done privately leaving his guests to surmise her identity. Then he would return with her on his arm after a sufficient time had passed.

As each attempt to uncover her was made, the audience became wilder with excitement. They were caught up with the teasing and seductive game that was being played in front of them. The cheers and ovations suddenly came to an abrupt halt when at long last Antipas grasped the end of the long golden ribbon belt of her toga.

Everyone seemed to struggle for breath as the anticipation mounted. As he tugged the long thread of cloth that covered her body, the dancer spun around and around in a circle leaving the golden ribbon to fly skyward when at long last her body was revealed. She stood before him naked except for the one thin golden piece of fabric still covering her face.

The crowd exploded with passionate gasps and applause as the golden dancer picked up one end of the ribbon to dance with it. Holding the silk high above her head, she spun the loose ends of the fabric making it coil back around her, covering her body once again. With a sharp turn she recoiled and exposed herself once again. Her bare feet slid from side to side as she slithered closer and closer to her prey. Her snakelike arms and hips waved almost hypnotically to the rhythm of the drums as she moved in for the kill.

All at once the audience suddenly began to chant, "Pull! Pull! Pull!" to encourage Antipas and to indicate to him how ravenous they were to know the identity of the dancer still hidden behind the golden veil. With dramatic flair she glided toward him in meek obedience, as if he possessed a power over her she could not stop. No one paid any attention to the silky golden veil as it dangled from Antipas' hand. Herod's reach had exposed the stunning beauty of his own stepdaughter, Salome.

Salome, princess from the royal lineage of Herod the Great, stood naked before him as the music abruptly ended. The crowd was silenced as they watched this exotic dance come to its dramatic close. As the the silky golden veil fell from Antipas' hand and the identity of the dancer penetrated the drunken minds of the guests, the whole assembly exploded in unrestrained applause.

The totally astonished Herod Antipas, smoldering with sexual passion, also had an obsessive need for approval and acceptance. The combination of the two events caused an intoxicating response. Having been invited to some of the foremost parties of the Roman Empire, none had surpassed this, which brought extreme satisfaction to his pride. The favorable responses of the most powerful men and women from the whole region far exceeded his wildest dreams. It seemed to confirm their acceptance of him in the coveted Roman social society that dominated Galilee.

As the party progressed, he was exhilarated when they tossed onto the dance floor tokens of their appreciation when each of the dancers' identities was revealed. This was considered high praise at any social function.

It was customary for hired entertainment to be tipped with additional financial favor if the esteemed host or his guests had found the performance exceptional. He had seen money, rings, or other jewelry thrown at the feet of performers as signs of approval in the past. However, this was like nothing he had ever seen before. The ground was literally covered with treasures, which increased with each unveiled dancer. His drunken thoughts were saturated with pride as he congratulated himself for being the cause of such an incredible party and having his guests entertained in such a wildly spectacular fashion.

Suddenly, as if all the blood that passionately surged through his veins only moments ago had rapidly stopped, a nagging question began to form in his mind. Trinkets of silver and gold would satisfy the performance of a hired dancer, but how did one reward the dance of a princess? All the things that made him puff with pride now came crashing down on him as protocol demanded satisfaction. It was totally scandalous for her to dance in public before an audience with men, let alone to appear naked. What was he to do? He was totally pleased by Salome's performance and indeed desired to reward her generously. To impress his guests, he could not offer the customary tip, as that would insult his stepdaughter in front of the renowned group.

Slowly he lifted his hands, gradually quieting the enthusiastic audience. Logic fought hard to penetrate through his inebriated state of mind. With a burst of sobriety, a clever plan was conceived.

Everyone was waiting for Herod to respond. "My dear Salome, your dance has indeed pleased me and the other esteemed guests tremendously," he paused for the clapping to subside. "Ask me for whatever you want, and I will give it to you," Herod bowed gallantly as he swore to her.

With that response, the audience went wild with enthusiasm and excitement. Getting caught up in the immediate acceptance of his guests, he again remarked, "Whatever you ask of me, I will give it to you, up to half of my kingdom" he promised.

No one clapped louder and with more enthusiasm than Herodias. At long last, her plans were finally coming together. Salome left the dance floor in a naked whirlwind. She found Herodias and asked of her, "What shall I ask for, Mother?"

With a ready answer, Herodias replied, "The head of John the Baptist."

Immediately, Salome ran from her mother back to her step-father, and before his guests she said, "Is it true you were indeed pleased with my dance and have promised me up to half your kingdom, dear...Father?" She hesitated long enough to find the correct title for her uncle, who was now her stepfather.

The guests' heads turned back and forth, looking from one to the other. There was little else for Herod Antipas to do but nod his agreement, having made his previous statement before so many witnesses.

"I want you to give to me at once the head of John the Baptist on a platter."

Wickedness begets more wickedness. Salome offered no objection when John's head was requested by her mother. In fact, she added her own sadistic part by requiring it to be served on a platter.

All eyes were again on Herod Antipas. What was he to do? He had already made an oath, and because of his dinner guests, he was unwilling to refuse her and be embarrassed.

Even through his drunken thoughts, knowing he could not back down, Herod was strangely sorry at the request. Sketchy memories of how he enjoyed listening to John flooded his thoughts. John was a strange man dressed in the wildest of clothes, but he seemed sincere when he told Herod of a new King and Kingdom that was out of this world. It was not unusual for people to want to hear new philosophies and new beliefs, and John's popularity was growing at an alarming rate. Although Herod considered John to be a holy and righteous man, he could not afford any problems or another troublemaker. He had had John arrested to appease Herodias, but he did not want him killed. He was superstitious and fearful that a murdered holy and righteous man could somehow do him harm or at best haunt him for the rest of his days. He had enough trouble as it was and did not want to risk more.

Antipas knew Herodias had nursed a grudge against John for speaking out against their marriage. Had she been so calculating, she could have arranged this whole party for such an end. Or was she trying to work through her daughter to secure the land he had inherited from his father, along with his wealth? Or could the answer be both? There were more pressing problems at hand so he could not think of that now.

The pounding of mugs on the tables expressed the guests' approval and awakened Herod from his weighty thoughts. Lust and excitement had created a powerful concoction within the hearts of those attending. Each guest had his or her own selfish desire to see Herod Antipas squirm. They were enjoying the fine mess Herodias had put Herod into and were anxious to see how he would save face. The roar of their drunken voices grew to a fevered pitch. Herod knew he had little choice.

"Executioner," he commanded, "do as she has requested."

CHAPTER 20

Silencing the Wilderness Crier

Samuel and Yaron finally made it to the great palace gardens. Yaron insisted upon seeing to the welfare of his daughters, no matter the condition of his knee. With a bandage as added support, he and Samuel had wormed their way though the city to find the meeting place Jahi had arranged earlier.

Just as they found a dark, secluded place to rest, marching soldiers exiting the palace portico with fierce determination could be heard as they made their way toward the palace prison. Jahi had found his way back to Samuel and reported the latest news from the banqueting hall.

"Not the head of John the Baptist!" Samuel and Yaron cried in disbelief. "No! No! No!" They said in unison.

Almost immediately the father and the son joined hands and prayed. Their prayers were comprised of protection for John and for the two girls caught up in this horrible drama. Samuel and Yaron beat their chests as the horror of the dramatic events played before their eyes.

"My precious daughters," Yaron mournfully cried and painfully added, "My precious friend."

"Oh, no," Abia's mouth uttered what her mind wanted to deny, "not John the Baptizer." Her thoughts were whirling. Evil was everywhere. There was no escaping it. How could something she believed to be as beautiful as dance become so wicked? What power of darkness had filled the minds and hearts of the dancers and those in the audience? How could dance be used to reward such evil with someone as good as John the Baptist? The questions that were forming in her brain were vain attempts to cope with what was currently happening.

What about Judith? What had she seen? What had she heard? Looking down at her sister resting in her lap, she realized Judith was still confused and dazed, but aware that something was definitely wrong. The wild applause and the banging of the goblets on the table had aroused Judith from her pain-filled sleep. As if in a dream too horrible to mention, Judith saw the nakedness of the dancer, she heard Salome's demented request, and saw the obedient guards as they marched only a few feet from the two of them. With whispers one had to strain to hear, Judith and Abia began to pray to God on John's behalf.

Fear began to grip their hearts like a vise. The reality of the situation and the need to escape collided. As if with one mind, Judith and Abia cautiously stood to their feet, hoping the current events would prevent them from being seen by any onlookers.

Abia had seen Jahi leave from the banqueting hall into a massive corridor on the right. It seemed to be the same direction the soldiers were taking. The guests began to form a long line as they headed for the prison to witness the beheading. People snaked past them on their way to satisfy their bloody, morbid curiosity. From a safe distance, the two sisters followed behind, turning and twisting their way out of the great banqueting hall. Timing was critical as they left the temporary shelter of hanging ribbons.

"Make way, make way!" came the shouts of the soldiers. Their cries caused the guests who had only just left the banqueting hall to press themselves against the cold walls of the great hall. An entry and exit line began to form. The executioner's steps were exaggerated and prideful as he marched past on the way to the prison along with the guards who flanked his sides.

Within minutes the executioner quickly returned. As if holding a prized stag, he clutched the head of John the Baptist with one fist and grasped the platter that carried John's head with the other.

At that moment Jahi grabbed both arms of the two girls from behind and pushed them from harm's way, but not before they caught glimpse of the familiar embroidered table covering now crudely cradling the head of the prophet, John.

CHAPTER 21

Days of Darkness and Light

The whole city tried desperately to recover from the shock and horror the incident had brought. Everyone seemed to be in a frenzy of uncertainty. Roman soldiers were at high alert. Jewish men tore their clothes and put ashes on their heads as they mourned John, who was one of their own. New believers of "The Way" were confused and apprehensive. Would they be next? What was to happen to them? Would John's message die with him? Rumors sprang forth from all directions; fear and panic were ready to spew like a bottle of cheap fermented wine.

Herod Antipas heard the reports about Jesus and the miracles He performed and was very frightened and very confused by them. Reports were coming to him from people with differing opinions of Jesus' true identity. "He is John the Baptist who has been raised from the dead," some said. Others said, "Elijah has come to us, or another prophet who lived long ago has risen from the dead!" His own guilty conscience and demonic superstition left Herod with no comfort. He had been used by satan to do his evil work and was now left to his own shame and self-destruction. Of this he had no clue.

Herod said, "I cut off John's head, so who is this man I hear such things about?" He wanted to see Jesus for himself, but was unable to do so because Jesus would not give him audience.

It was said that John's disciples came and took away John's body to give him a proper burial. When Jesus was informed of John's death, Jesus departed from them all to be alone for a while. He was grieved at heart because of the tragic death of His cousin and because wicked rulers over Israel had killed yet another prophet sent by God. Everyone, including Jesus, wondered what impact John's death would have on the people and what effect it would have for Jesus and His ministry. The Jewish people were like children, as if suddenly orphaned by violent acts of war. Who would take care of them? What were they to do?

When Jesus returned, He saw the multitudes arrive in search of Him the day after John was beheaded. Jesus was filled with a deep love and was moved by compassion for the people. He went to them and healed the sick, comforted the hurting, and consoled each grieving heart.

The mass gathering of people continued until it was evening. The people were coming and going in a state of violent emotional upheaval, and Jesus and His apostles were left with no time to eat. Jesus advised the apostles to get away by themselves for some rest. So they got in a boat and went off to a remote place by themselves for a while.

A short time later, His apostles came back to Jesus to ask Him to send the people away so they could go into the villages and buy food for themselves. Jesus insisted the people did not have to go away to get something to eat. The disciples looked dismayed at the five loaves and two fish they had with them, never dreaming what would happen next.

Jesus had the people sit down in the grass as He looked up to Heaven. He blessed and broke the bread and fish. The disciples took the pieces and fed the multitudes, leaving 12 baskets full of fragments. Five thousand men, besides women and children, were fed that day. Jesus said the people reminded Him of sheep without a shepherd, and He immediately started to guide and teach them.

Time seemed to pour forth as slowly as honey on a cold morning. One day eventually gave way to another as the Ben-David family tried to put together the very perplexing riddle of what they had had the misfortune of witnessing. For several days, it seemed as if everyone in the family silently agreed not to speak of Herod's birthday celebration, the entrapment of Judith and Abia, and John's beheading. If only the emotional trauma could be healed as quickly as Yaron's knee.

When Jahi appeared at their door, everyone could ignore the subject no longer. With a humble bow, Jahi's eyes portrayed his thankfulness that everyone was safe and together again. Samuel and Yaron ushered him in with grateful hearts as well. As they gathered around the warm fire, the mysteries of that night unfolded as each piece of a puzzle began to form a picture.

That fateful night, Samuel and Yaron had anxiously awaited word from Jahi, searching every face in the crowd for his. The soldiers marched past them on their way to the prison for the head of John the Baptist. Great crowds of people were gathering in the gardens, hoping to catch the first glimpse of the murdered victim.

Yaron saw the executioner coming from the prison and motioned for Samuel to take advantage of the chaotic situation to enter the palace in search of Judith and Abia. It was discovered that certain areas of the palace were unguarded, so as fast as Yaron's throbbing knee would allow, they inched onward.

Giant pillars of marble became their refuge for occasional rest and to ensure their further safety. It was behind one such pillar that they found Jahi, safely holding his two very frightened wards. When finally Abia saw her father and brother, she surrendered to the blissful darkness that had threatened to overtake her time and time again.

Jahi waited with them as the crowd moved back into the banqueting hall following the wicked processional. Jahi carried Judith and Samuel carried Abia to the safety of their home. Jahi had risked his own life to help them, and the tears of the whole family glistened their recognition and gratitude of the fact. Jahi's small stature seemed to gain size as the family's heart appreciation reached his.

Never had Jahi been treated with such kindness and respect. They did not seem to notice he was a slave, but saw him as a man. He did not know why this family was so different from others he had known, but he wondered if it had something to do with the man who had died and the Jewish man, Jesus, whom they followed. As he made his way toward the door, he determined to find out more about this family and the God they served.

In the days to come, Jahi became a frequent visitor to the Ben-David family. They befriended him and taught him about Jesus. As a result, Jahi, became a believer in Jesus. He brought many others into the faith within the confines of the palace walls. His station in life did not change, he remained a slave in the household of Herod, but for the first time in his whole life, he was free.

CHAPTER 22

So They Can Be Sound in Their Faith

It is said that time heals all wounds. Judith and Abia discovered that only God can heal wounds, and time only makes one gradually forget the enormity of the memory of the wounds. The memories of the sights, smells, and behaviors witnessed that frightful night fit into both of those categories.

Papa told them that all things seem to grow bigger in the dark and that they should not keep their feelings hidden in darkness, but rather surrender them to the light. Judith and Abia found it became easier to talk about the things they had seen as time traveled onward.

Abia's thoughts were consumed with questions that could not be explained naturally. As a five-year-old girl, Abia had dreamed of a woman who was very wicked dressed in gold who danced. Why had she been warned in a dream of such a dancer 12 years ago? For what purpose did God have her witness such evil, and why could she not get the wicked dance out of her mind? For now, all she had were questions with very few answers.

To say the Ben-Davids were the same after surviving such an event would only be a lie. The fiercely-guarded innocence of the world in which they lived came crashing down on that day. They had witnessed history in the making, and it was not a pretty picture to them anymore.

The old stories of the past and the retelling of tremendous historical events of their ancient Hebrew ancestors had been painted in such heroic and sterile ways. Time had far removed the pain, the blood, and the sting of their history. However, those events had unfurled just as the ones they experienced had. The day started out with the predictable, the expected, and the commonplace—but what a difference a few hours could make.

Just as in the days of old, people tried to make sense of their circumstances. Everyone tried to bring order in the midst of such chaos. Yaron explained to his family that, unfortunately, they had been caught up in a deadly political game played by selfish, self-indulgent people whose only ambition was lust for power and who sought that power by political gains, financial means, military strength, or social clout. Every event on that dreadful day had some type of natural explanation to satisfy normal intelligence.

The political and religious upheavals continued in all of Galilee, Samaria, Perea, Judea, and other nearby regions. Sides were being drawn. Neighbor was turning against neighbor and family against family. A distinct line was being drawn that separated the followers of "The Way"—those who were believers in Jesus as the long-awaited Messiah in accordance with John's teaching—and those who thought it to be complete heresy.

These were days of great distress, but also days of fantastic miracles and extraordinary healings. Incredible stories of Jesus' teachings and miracles spread like wildfires. Many accounts of Jesus were being spread far and wide. One could not go to the marketplace or the synagogue without Jesus and the disciples being discussed at great length. The stories were unbelievable, yet people had seen with their own eyes the healings and other impossible feats. Of this fact, Abia was very much aware since He had healed her almost a year ago beside the dusty road to Jerusalem, when He called her His dancer.

Jesus, Jesus, Jesus. His stories were the topic of heated debate for the skeptical, but fuel for the flame of the faithful. Jesus had already fed 5,000 with five loaves and two fish. Lazarus was raised from death by Jesus. Jesus walked on the water. He could forgive and heal. He proclaimed Himself to be the Son of God. Jesus defended women and healed small children. There were even stories of demoniacs being healed from the demons that possessed them. Forgiveness, love, and God's grace were being discussed. Blind, lame, and deaf people were restored. His miracles were spectacular, and the change enacted in people's hearts was the greatest miracle of all.

Jesus walked humbly with people and treated both the rich and poor with dignity and respect. He modeled how people are to serve and have a servant's heart toward others. He was in constant communion with God the Father and taught others how to pray. His style of leadership was gentle, but when necessary, He confronted evil or evil deeds. In all He did, He brought glory to God and took no credit for His deeds, yet He was confident in the authority God had given Him.

The Pharisees and Sadducees were challenged and defeated by Jesus' voice of authority and power. They became enraged and alleged that Jesus had made fools of the common people because they knew nothing about Jewish law. Being experts, they would never be taken in by such a charlatan. Angered by the growing numbers who followed Jesus because of the miracles He was doing and because He dared to say He was God's Son, some of the Jews picked up stones to stone Jesus. Others attempted to put Him in jail.

The most religious of men quarreled over the Kingdom of God and God's judgment that was to come. While Jesus stilled the raging sea, people argued about whether Jesus was a prophet or if He was the Christ. While Jesus healed people on the Sabbath and taught about spiritual blindness, others bickered over human traditions and customs versus God's Law.

Jesus was rejected by many, although He taught about God the Father as a loving father waiting on the prodigal son's return. So it went, one story after another, either increasing people's faith or confirming to others a travesty. Yet, the miracles continued.

Jesus began to warn those who followed His teaching that there would be danger ahead for them. He predicted His own betrayal and troubled times ahead. He foretold His own death, resurrection, and second coming. To the apostles He explained that only His departure would allow the Helper or the Holy Spirit to come to convict the world concerning sin and righteousness and judgment. He reassured them that they would not be left as orphans.

The Ben-David family followed Jesus, and wherever He taught publicly, they went to hear Him. Yaron and Samuel sat under His teaching at the synagogue. They were constantly astounded at the love and compassion of His ministry; yet He held such authority that even the most powerful trembled and were amazed.

Everyone began to notice the lack of tolerance many had toward Jesus and His new teachings. Jesus and His doctrines made many secret and blatant enemies. Death threats were an almost daily occurrence.

Followers of Jesus heard strange reports that Jesus had spoken of His own death on three different occasions. Yet, all thoughts of Jesus dying seemed far removed because He brought so much excitement, love, healing, and grace everywhere He went.

CHAPTER 23

The Sounds of Obedience

It had been almost two years since John the Baptist's death, and it was approaching Jesus' third Passover since His ministry had begun. In the springtime, a few days before the Passover Feast, Jesus went to Bethany. Simon, the Leper, was giving a dinner in Jesus' honor. Lazarus and his two sisters, Mary and Martha, were attending. They were very close friends with Jesus, and their home was His whenever He was in Jerusalem.

Martha helped serve the food at the dinner party. While the men were reclining, having completed their meal, Mary approached Jesus with a pint of very expensive spikenard, a fragrant oil used for burial. She had heard Jesus tell of His death and believed Him, although some of the disciples refused to accept what He was saying. She poured the perfume on Jesus' feet to prepare Him for burial. While the sweet smell filled the whole house, she wiped His feet with her hair as an act of worship and appreciation for raising her brother from the dead and as a way to express her love and devotion to Him.

Judas Iscariot, one of Jesus' disciples, criticized Mary for being so wasteful when the poor could have used the money, although he took money from the money bag regularly. Jesus reprimanded him and said that what she did was a beautiful thing. Judas' heart became enraged, and he plotted to do evil to Jesus.

A large number of Jews heard Jesus was in Bethany. They wanted to see Him and Lazarus, whom Jesus had raised from the dead. Many people were deserting the Jews and starting to believe in Jesus because of the great miracle that had been done to Lazarus. The leading priests made plans to kill Lazarus, and Caiaphas, the high priest of the Jews, also wanted Jesus dead. It seemed to him the whole world was following Jesus, and he was extremely jealous. However, Caiaphas did not want Jesus to be arrested yet because of the large numbers of people who were gathering in Jerusalem for the Passover Feast. He feared a riot would break out in protest if any action was taken against Him.

Many people had heard Jesus was traveling the two miles from Bethany to attend the Passover Feast and were excited about His coming. Jesus told two of His disciples to go ahead of Him and told them exactly where to get a donkey for Him to ride as He entered Jerusalem. If anyone objected, they were to say, "The Lord has need of it." When Jesus arrived, He found the people on the road waiting to pay tribute and to honor Him.

The Ben-David family, having heard about Jesus' plans to come back to Jerusalem, arrived just in time to be among those who had the privilege of honoring Jesus as He entered the city. Yaron and Hannah took their place along the long dusty road that led into Jerusalem. Judith, having been a married woman for over a year, was there with her beloved Abraham and the rest of the Ben-Daniel family. Judith's mother-in-law, Mora, was busy spreading the good news about Abraham and Judith's baby, who would be born in the early winter.

Samuel came with his parents, but soon found his place beside Abia's best friend, Mary. At long last, Samuel had asked Mary to become his wife, and she was soon to become the newest member of the Ben-David family in the summer.

Scanning the roadside the Ben-Davids could see many familiar faces standing with palm tree branches in hand waiting for Jesus to pass by, but unfortunately many did not gather. There were a great number of people who had been healed by Jesus' touch who did not bother to come to welcome Jesus back into the city.

Regrettably, others did not come for other reasons. Akil, head social planner to the palace, paid the Ben-Davids a visit to give to Yaron what was owed to him for his services. He thanked Yaron and his family for the spectacular fabric craftsmanship, and the payment for their hard work was more than generous. Akil also brought bad news. Jahi, the slave to King Herod and a beloved friend of the Ben-David family, had been murdered by another palace slave who took great offense when Jahi tried to speak to him about Jesus. Jahi, before he died, reported that he had found boldness to speak about Jesus to others, and he even witnessed to Akil about Jesus. Akil admitted to being indifferent and wanted no part of religion in any form, but said it was indeed unfortunate about Jahi, for he was an adequate slave.

The family was very much saddened by the news of Jahi's death, but he was not the only friend of the Ben-Davids who had recently died. Yaron's old friend Malachi was found dead in his bed by Hannah and Yaron, who had been paying him a visit to share with him some warm soup and fresh bread. Jahi and Malachi would have loved to be a part of today's festivities to honor Jesus and were sorely missed.

As the crowd gathered, some planned to wave palm tree branches high in the air when Jesus passed them by. Other followers planned to pave the street with their coats to honor Him. The sick and the afflicted lined the streets as well, hoping Jesus would reach out to touch them and heal them as He passed.

Suddenly, Samuel's friend, Benjamin, came running down the road ahead of Jesus shouting, "He's coming! He's coming!"

Abia could hold back no longer. With tambourines in both hands lifted high into the air, she began to spin and twirl in pure delight with the approach of her healer and Lord. Some of the other girls joined her as they made a giant circle in the center of the road. They danced to the shouts and songs of jubilation as Jesus approached, seated on the back of a donkey. "Praise God! God bless the One who comes in the name of the Lord! God bless the King of Israel! Blessed be the name of our Lord, Jesus, the Messiah!" The crowds watched Jesus enter the kingdom of Jerusalem as though He were the King and they His loyal subjects.

"Hosanna! Hosanna! Hosanna!" the people began to shout out in unison. The sound was incredibly loud and spirited. As He crossed the threshold onto the street paved by the coats and palm branches of His followers, some of the sick began to shout as well. Some shouted, "I'm healed!" while others shouted "I have been made whole!"

As Abia worshiped Jesus with her dancing and people on the streets were getting healed of their "hurts," it became apparent that another one of her dreams had come true.

This event had been prophesied by the prophet Zechariah hundreds of years ago. By openly coming into the city on a donkey, Jesus was now a marked man. The Jewish leaders detested Him for the supposition that He was the fulfillment of Zechariah's prophecy. The flame of hatred and resentment growing within the hearts of the most religious burned uncontrollably, and they frantically looked for the only outlet acceptable—the death of Jesus.

At the sight of Jerusalem and the people He loved, Jesus cried tears of sadness and spoke about Jerusalem's future for having rejected their King and the salvation He offered them. God had not rejected them, but they rejected Him.

When Jesus entered the Temple, He began to drive out those who were making lots of money. They charged an extra Temple tax, overcharged for sacrificial animals, and shortchanged foreigners who came to the Temple for worship. The moneychangers' and merchants' stalls and tables were placed in the Temple in such a way as to intentionally block the entry of the Gentiles, or non-Jews, who came to worship God. They had made the Temple into a robbers' den. With righteous indignation Jesus overturned the tables and declared, *"My house shall be called a house of prayer for all nations!"*

Throughout the time of the Feast, Jesus entered the Temple daily and taught all who had gathered many things. He taught mysteries about how He was in the Father and the Father was in Him. He said that those who believed would do greater works of healings than the miracles they had seen Him do. Jesus said He was going back to the Father in Heaven. Those who knew Jesus' character and will could ask the Father anything by using Jesus' name; they would receive if they loved Him and kept His commandments.

No longer would only prophets, priests, and kings have access to the Holy Spirit, as in days of the past. But the Spirit of Truth, another Helper who was equal to Jesus, would come and be with all people who believed in Jesus. The Helper would teach about all things and bring Jesus' teachings to the believers' remembrance. Jesus was leaving Earth to go back to his Father, and He did not want His people to be afraid. The Holy Spirit of Peace was to be given to those who believed in Him and loved Him. This gift of the Holy Spirit could not come until Jesus laid down His life for Jews and Gentiles alike, His friends.

Jesus modeled the sacrificial love and service that were requirements of the new Kingdom of God. He served warnings that the world would hate those who testified about Him and who followed His teachings, just as they hated Him. In fact, He said those who killed the followers of Jesus would believe they were offering a service to God. But the Holy Spirit would keep believers from stumbling, and He would convict the world concerning sin and righteousness and judgment. He would guide and direct followers of Jesus into all truth. All things the Father had given to Jesus would be given to those who loved, belonged to, and had faith in Jesus. They would have what He had.

Although in the world there would be great tribulation and troubles, He encouraged everyone to take courage, for Jesus would overcome the world and the rulers of the world. Jesus prayed for Himself and for His disciples and all future believers. He had made the Father's name known to the people and expressed how the Father loved Him, but in a day yet to come, Jesus would be in the people, and they could know the love the Father has for them.

Jesus' third Passover meal since His ministry began approached, and He sent Peter and John ahead to prepare the Passover meal for Him and His disciples. Not knowing where to prepare the Passover meal, they asked Jesus. He replied by instructing them to go into the city where a man would meet them carrying a pitcher of water; they should follow him into the house he would enter. Because women were usually the ones who carried water, it was easy for them to spot the man. He showed Peter and John into a large, furnished upper room of his house where he left them to prepare the meal.

Jesus met with His disciples in the upper room to celebrate. Jesus knew that it was time for Him to leave this world and go back to the Father in Heaven. Jesus told the 12 that one of them would betray Him, yet He washed their feet with a towel before they ate. Of course, the idea that someone would betray Jesus seemed ridiculous, and not one admitted it. Jesus told Judas He knew he was the one who was to give Him over to the chief priests and officers, who had offered to pay him 30 pieces of silver for his consent and help.

Jesus also told Peter that he would deny knowing Jesus three times before the rooster crowed that day. He told Peter that He had prayed for him that his faith would not fail and that shame would not keep him from returning back to his brothers. Peter would be used to strengthen them against the temptation to deny Jesus themselves. Peter could not believe he would do such a thing, pledging that he was willing to go to prison and face death if need be on behalf of Jesus.

Jesus gave thanks for the bread and wine. He shared with them the bread, saying that it was His body and that the wine was His blood. His blood would be a covenant for the forgiveness of sins. His body would be given up for the benefit of all. Such things were mysteries. Throughout the meal Jesus spoke with an urgency and passion as never before. The conversation seemed painful to Him, as if there was not enough time to convey all the love in His heart. After the Passover meal was over, the group sang hymns of praise to God for His goodness and faithfulness.

They left the upper room and went for a walk to a peaceful spot among a grove of olive trees at the foot of the Mount of Olives. It was a place often frequented by Jesus, and a place He sought when He wanted to get away to pray; it was called the Garden of Gethsemane.

Jesus asked the disciples to sit down and wait for Him until He finished praying. Peter, James, and John were asked to go with Him a little farther. Jesus was very disturbed and troubled, and He told the three He felt His soul was so deeply grieved that He was to the point of death. Peter, James, and John were instructed to pray and keep watch while Jesus went a little farther away to pray alone.

Groans and screams could be heard in the darkness of the night as He fell to the ground overcome with emotions. He expressed them to His Father, "My Father, if it is possible, let this cup of suffering be taken away from Me." Jesus knew what lay ahead of Him and the horrifying death facing Him. He did not want to be crucified if another way was possible.

"Oh, My Father, not My will, but Yours be done," Jesus said, conceding His will to the Father's. Dying was an important legal action that had to be done in order for God's people to be ransomed, redeemed, justified, saved, reconciled, and adopted. Jesus' blood would satisfy and cover the sins of the world.

An angel from Heaven appeared to Him and strengthened Him, but the agony continued as He prayed. Three times Jesus went back to His disciples, only to find them asleep, unable to keep their eyes open. For more than three hours Jesus prayed fervently until His sweat became like drops of blood covering His face and dripping upon the ground.

When He rose from His prayers, Jesus went back to His disciples and awakened them once again to tell them of the approaching mob of people armed with swords, clubs, and lanterns, for it was already night. The mob had been sent by the leading Jewish priests and other leaders of the people, and along with them came a Roman cohort of soldiers. Judas, one of the 12 disciples, was with them, and he greeted Jesus with a kiss. This kiss was the signal Judas used to betray Jesus. At that point, all the disciples fled and deserted Him just as Jesus had prophesied earlier.

The Roman cohort, the commander, and the officers of the Jews arrested Jesus and had Him tied up. They took Him to Annas, who had been high priest of the Jews until the Roman government removed him from the position and his son-in-law, Caiaphas, took his place. Many Jews still considered him to be their leader, so they took Jesus to Annas first. Annas found no grounds for charging Jesus of any crime during a pretrial hearing late that same night. He passed Jesus on to his son-in-law, Caiaphas. Jesus was then brought before the Sanhedrin, the supreme court for the Jews. It was made up of 70 men picked among fellow Jews to handle civil, criminal, and religious cases. The president of the Sanhedrin was the high priest, Caiaphas.

Caiaphas was one of the high priests who was afraid of the growing influence Jesus had on the people who were following Him. Caiaphas was said to have organized a plot to kill Jesus. When that did not work, he began to trump up false evidence to frame Jesus. Jesus remained silent when Caiaphas interrogated Him, demanding Jesus say whether He was the Messiah, the long-awaited Jewish king. Caiaphas charged Jesus with blasphemy and for claiming He was the Messiah. But the Sanhedrin could not execute convicted criminals; only the Roman government could. For that reason, Caiaphas sent Jesus to Pontius Pilate, the Roman governor of Judea, insisting Jesus be executed for His crimes. Jesus was sent to Pilate badly beaten by orders of Caiaphas, the supposed leader of God's people.

"Are you King of the Jews?" Pilate asked Jesus.

Jesus answered him, "Are you saying this on your own initiative, or did others tell you about Me?"

Pilate said to Jesus, "I am not a Jew, am I? Your own people and chief priests delivered You to me. So You are a king?"

"It is as you say, but My Kingdom is not of this world," Jesus answered Pilate.

Pilate proclaimed to the Jews who were gathered there that Jesus was not guilty of any crime. He thought he would punish

Him and then release Him, but the crowd's insatiable appetite for death was set. It was Passover time, and as was customary, one prisoner would be released from a death sentence. Not wanting to be the one to take the blame for Jesus' death, Pilate, however, decided to put the responsibility on the people instead. When given a choice between Jesus and a criminal, the crowd picked the criminal to be released instead of the innocent One who had healed, encouraged, and loved them.

"No, crucify Him!" the crowd insisted.

Pilate wanted no part of sentencing an innocent man, so when he had heard that Jesus was a Galilean, he gave orders for Him to be sent to Herod Antipas, in whose jurisdiction Jesus belonged. Pilate had Jesus scourged with a three-pronged whip. Before being sent to Herod Antipas, Jesus suffered again at the hands of the Roman soldiers, who made fun of Him, twisted together a crown of thorns to put on His head, and put a purple robe upon His back. They put a reed in Jesus' right hand and then mockingly knelt down before Him, saying, "Hail, King of the Jews!" Then they spat on Him and took from His hand the reed and began to beat Him on the head. They ripped the purple robe off Him and put His own garments back on Him, finally sending Him to Herod.

Herod Antipas, the very one who had John the Baptist killed, had wanted to see Jesus for quite some time. He thought Jesus could entertain him with His miracles and wonders. Herod Antipas, the want-to-be-king, questioned the true King with many words, but Jesus gave him no answers. So Herod Antipas and his men of war treated Him with contempt, mocked Him, and beat Him. With the same dramatic flair used at his birthday banquet, Herod further mocked Jesus by clothing Him in a royal purple robe, and he sent Him so dressed back to Pilate.

The early morning streets were thronged with people running chaotically in all directions to report to their families and friends what was happening to Jesus. The men in the marketplace had gathered together outside the gates of the royal palace when they heard Jesus had been taken to Herod Antipas. Desiring to find out for themselves what was going on and to lend any type of support they could for Jesus, they got there just in time to find that the soldiers were on their way to take Jesus back to Pilate.

Among the men who had gathered at the royal gates were Yaron and Samuel, along with about ten others. When they saw Jesus, they could hardly believe their eyes. His face was so bloodied from the cruel treatment of Antipas' soldiers that they hardly recognized Him. They were helpless against the military force that flanked both sides of Jesus and could do nothing but watch Him pass. Samuel and Yaron were horror-struck when they recognized the now faded and blood-soaked royal purple robe as the one they had sewn for Herod Antipas a few years earlier.

Hannah and Abia somehow found Yaron and Samuel among the swelling crowds. Sprinkled within the hate-filled crowd were many fellow believers in Jesus—fighting their way through the crowds of people who had come to mock and disrespect Jesus. As horrendous as the situation was, they felt they had to be near to Jesus, even if it meant witnessing once again the horrors of another innocent man being slain.

The crucifixion was horrible and so tragic. Jesus had already explained to His followers about His death and how it must happen. The cross represented sin that separated humankind from God. The penalty for sin is death. In order for sin to be removed, blood had to be shed. Instead of people dying, God had allowed animals to die in their place. But the sacrificial system was not enough, so Jesus had come as a spotless Lamb, a sacrifice to once and for all redeem people back to God. "Behold, the Lamb of

God who takes away the sins of the world," John the Baptist had once said.

Abia wept bitter tears when she realized that everything she was about to see was for her benefit. The prophet Isaiah had said there would be a perfect sacrifice that would be wounded for the transgressions and bruised for the iniquities of others. *Oh, my God,* she began to realize, *the perfect sacrifice is my friend Jesus!*

The savage and inhumane crucifixion of Jesus was horrendous, yet as she watched, Abia saw something much more. It was like a dance between two partners—one good and the other evil. As tragic and horrifying as Jesus' death dance was, it was something else, too; there would be terrible greatness as a result of His dance.

CHAPTER 24

For the Joy Set Before Him, He Endured the Dance

From the His earliest memory, Jesus had worked with wood in his earthly father's carpenter shop. His calloused hands had been accustomed to skillfully taking a piece of wood and crafting it into something beautiful. He could make and repair objects and structures that only a knowledgeable woodworker could.

Now, as He approached the moment of crucifixion, His experienced eye assessed the wood that lay at His feet. Certainly, He had no experience with this type of rough plank. From its appearance, it was a piece of wood that any carpenter would have easily rejected, but *no*. There was something inside this old piece of hard wood. Held captive inside the long timber was the shape of a dancer that only His eyes could see. She needed a partner to make her into the image of what He saw. From the look of her unyielding position within the wood that encased her, the work would be tremendously difficult for Him. This unwilling dance partner was much more than a hardened object of wood; she was a picture of His mission to bring life back to all the hardened souls who would one day become His Bride.

With His heart beating wildly within His chest, Jesus cast His swollen eyes to the ground where she lay. Her crossbeam arms were stiff and unyielding. Her length was a little longer than the width of a grown man's outstretched arms. Her leaves and branches of former beauty and glory had been stripped from her, leaving her with only a trunk. Centuries of disgrace and the humiliation of her sins had left her trunk stained through and through with reminders of her past. The food of resentment, hatred, shame, guilt, apathy, pride, offense, disgust, and many other poisons had passed through her roots, causing bitterness to be lodged in her heart-wood, making it inflexible. It pulsed with hostility.

Generational sins thought to be underground and hidden made her exhausted and hard. Her inner bark was blackened by the sins of others and the sins she had imposed on others. Her own attempts to protect herself had made her outer bark non-responsive and indignant to all efforts made by others to help her. Distrust, mistrust, unbelief, and strong suspicion made her guarded and unapproachable. She weighed at least 125 pounds, and she was full of attitudes, beliefs, and mindsets that were so twisted that she blamed others for her obesity.

Vowing to never be a victim again, she had now become the opposite: the prey. Her arms were outstretched. She offered her-self to others in an attempt to heal the pain. Sin and satan worked as partners to entice the wounded with fleeting relief, empty promises, lies, and deferred hope. Then, when she was once again humiliated and tricked by the same old lines, satan laughed at her and it brought more pain. She believed his lies about her, and to self-medicate from the pain, she turned once again to anything and anyone who could offer her false help.

She hated and was hated; she looked for a way out, but the only voice she heard was the one who wanted her harmed or killed. Satan patiently watched her self-destruct. He did not want to be accused of murder, but if he could convince her that any other voice of love, acceptance, and forgiveness was wrong, she would kill herself. Either way he would win.

Satan saw God's precious creation—humankind—bowing down in worship to him and rejecting the Creator's wisdom, help, and truth as a victory in and of itself. The God of love and hope having hopeless and loveless children was sweet success to the enemy of humanity and humanity's God.

Jesus saw His wooden-hearted dance partner and reached for her, regardless of her outward and inward appearance. He was a willing partner, not a forced one. With outstretched arms He picked her up from the dirt in which she seemed determined to stay.

With a pout and a show of displeasure, she seemed resolute to make this dance as difficult as possible. She was indifferent to Him and the help He offered her. She would be heavy and lazy and would hinder Him any chance she could. It was as if all the evil in the world were gathered together to keep this dance from occurring. Despite her resistance, Jesus bowed from the waist and embraced His wooden crossbeam dance partner. This was a dance He was created and destined for.

At long last, He lifted her to His shoulder to support her as they moved onward down the Via Delarosa. Jesus was not ashamed to be seen with her and paraded her in front of the people who were gathering around both sides of their dance floor. The cross silently showed the audience their ugly sins—the ones He was carrying for them. He was rewarded with angry shouts and malicious gazes. Only a few people seemed to recognize what Jesus was doing and were in agony for being the cause of it.

The weight of the people's sins made the tree heavier and heavier as time went by. He carried it anyway. He seemed to be devoted to carrying it no matter its appearance or the shame He was incurring. This was to be a slow dance, a very slow dance.

From one place to another He carried her. People began to circle around the tragic couple as if enjoying His struggle and heartbreak. As the dance proceeded, they bumped into the people on the crowded narrow street of the dance floor. His off-balance dance steps amused some while sickening others. He embraced His wooden dance partner with both hands, leading her all the while to Golgotha, the Place of the Skull.

Inch by inch they moved to the rhythmic beat of the soldiers' whips and the chaotic roar of the audience. Cheek to cheek, He led his reluctant partner upward and onward to the summit of the Skull.

Astounded onlookers who gawked at the couple from both sides of the road wondered where He got His inspiration for this dance. Desperately He fought to hold her and to protect her from returning to the dirt and mire she came from. Yet she seemed equally determined to return there. She put splinters into His hands, arms, and legs as His reward for dancing with her.

The new and old blood mixed together as it spilled over the hardened body of wood. His blood of forgiveness flowed into the deepest crevices of her unbendable, wooden inner being. No sin was left uncovered. Each and every sin she could ever commit in the past, present, and future was included. His open crimson wounds covered all transgressions, while the hidden and secret iniquities were covered by the dark purple pools of blood which bruised His body beneath His skin.

Her refusal and resistance to participate in the dance seemed to be understood by Jesus. He knew this dance would save people from eternal death and damnation, but the enemies of God were stubbornly heartless. In protest, she spun and dodged His grip, but He compassionately gained control, as if steadying a rebellious child. Did she not realize He was not going to give up? Nothing was going to discourage Him or prevent Him from finishing this dance. His passion and uninhibited movements seemed to communicate a type of love and sacrifice never before seen.

God so loved the world that He gave Jesus, His only Son, to save the world from their sins, to give all who believe in Him eternal life and a restored relationship with God the Father. Jesus' love for His Father and love for the world made Him more determined than ever. He was not going to sit this dance out.

Jesus' dance was dramatic at times as His movements were strong and sure. At others, everyone wondered if one foot would indeed follow the other. How could He go on?

Then the inevitable happened. He fell, dropping His companion with a thud. All of Heaven and hell seemed to strain to see what would happen next. The human-made crown of humiliation went tumbling on the dusty road. The Roman soldiers were filled with distaste and contempt as they watched this ridiculous dance.

Thinking Jesus would not be able to carry on, they grabbed another man from the crowd to take His place. Simon of Cyrene assumed Jesus' stance with the weight of Jesus' partner resting fully on him. With the crown now tightly put back onto Jesus' head, Jesus was ordered to walk alone. His wooden partner and Simon followed Jesus' steps onward and upward. They did not dance very far when Simon's strength was waning.

One of the Roman soldiers insisted on cutting in on the dance once again. He ordered Simon to give Jesus' partner back to Him. Jesus' blood, sweat, and tears covered the long wooden body of His dance partner. It seemed as if being away from her hurt Him more than dancing with her. Simon wondered how Jesus could be so determined to get her back when he was so relieved to be rid of such an ugly and reluctant dance partner.

At first it seemed as though Jesus was being ordered to dance by the soldiers, but the look in His eyes when they handed the cross back to Him seemed to suggest quite the opposite. Jesus once again reached out to His pathetic dance partner as if clinging to her in a desperate and loving embrace.

Simon bowed from the waist in respect and awe of the man whose strength, purpose, and commitment he did not understand. How could Jesus want to resume the ghastly dance he was thankfully free from? This was not something he could do. Only Jesus could carry the weight of that cross. Simon knew he could not have carried the weight of his own sins upon the cross, let alone the sins of the whole world. Only Jesus could bring redemption and sanctification to this dance.

Simon stood a safe distance away from the dance floor as the two passed him by once again. Admiration and gratitude filled his thoughts as he watched the procession.

The divine dance proceeded with repeated turns and spins. The pattern of movements seemed to vary, and at times it seemed like Jesus would not be able to continue. Jesus was bloody from the whipping and harsh treatment of the soldiers. Long splinters kept lodging under His skin, making His appearance more repulsive than ever.

The stripes upon His back for every known and unknown sickness were taking their toll. Every inflammation, affliction, infirmity, sickness, disease, disorder, syndrome, abnormal cell, cyst, radical cell, abnormal growth, blood condition, stress, lesion, metastasizing cell, swelling, discomfort, bone pain, depression, nausea, fatigue, and spasm from every organ or bone in the body, He carried.

His mind was invaded by evil thoughts, and deeds from the pit of hell were made known to Him. Unclean, evil, deceitful, seducing, lying, antichrist, religious, familiar, perverse, medium, and slumbering spirits assaulted His mind with knowledge of slavery, bondages, fear, infirmity, heaviness, haughtiness, harlotry, whoredom, divination, distortion, error, stupor, and jealousy. Scenes of the destruction and violence of humankind filled His mind. Yet, He danced on.

In unity, Jesus and His ungraceful partner stood, stumbled, and fell, causing Him to once again strain to stand. She continued to offer Him no assistance and seemed to laugh when her efforts caused Him to stagger and trip.

Her expressed amusement was hushed as He continued to be the leader of the dance. Over and over again she thought she had victory over Him, but with every fiber of His being He forged ahead.

They bobbed up and down and twisted about until the sadistic music of the crowd came to an abrupt halt. Once again the military leaders in charge of the dance ripped Jesus' partner from Him. This time, they threw her down onto the ground and made Jesus lie with His bloody back next to her as they nailed His feet and hands to her. They hung a mocking sign above His head proclaiming Him to be King of the Jews.

Grief-stricken women and men began to shout questions at the cruel soldiers as the hammering increased. "Are you afraid you will have to take Jesus' place and dance with His hideous partner?" "Can't you tell by now how dedicated He is to finishing this dance Himself?" "Why must you nail Him to the cross?" "Are you afraid Jesus would not hold out long enough to finish this dance to its end?"

Not quite sure if the words were spoken aloud or not, Jesus thought, *I will finish this dance. I was born for it. For you, My Bride, I will finish this dance, though it will kill Me.*

When the soldiers offered Jesus a drink of sour wine, He refused. No wine would touch His lips until that glorious day when He would return for His Bride. The Father God wanted a family, and the Son of God wanted a Bride. This death dance promised by the Father would guarantee the fulfillment of these desires. Jesus' shed blood would be for the forgiveness of His Bride's sins; the stripes on His back would be for her healing; and the ugly cross He danced with would keep her from having to suffer the curse her sin would incur. His humiliation would allow her to know Him in a way never yet known. If only she would have faith in Him, this dance would not be in vain.

Gently, Jesus leaned His weary head against the old, wooden cross as His thoughts drifted to the day when His reward, His Bride, would be presented to Him by His Father. He could see her even now, without spot or blemish, due to the finished dance with the cross. It was worth all the pain and suffering He was going through.

This dance was to His death, but it would bring His Bride new life. He would gladly dance with this dreadful cross in exchange for the dance they would share at the Marriage Supper of the Lamb. One day His Bride would be as eager to dance with Him as He was to dance with her.

He proceeded in the dance until His last breath was spent, and with that last breath He declared, "It is finished." For His last dance movement, He bowed His head in a silent salute and gave up His spirit, so she, His Bride, in the near future, could have His Spirit and live.

What the first Adam did not do, the second Adam, Jesus, accomplished. As the blood and water flowed out of His side from the soldier's jab with a spear, Jesus' Bride, the redeemed Church, was born.

CHAPTER 25

A Time to Mourn
and a Time to Dance

Never would Abia view dance in the same way again. Salome's dance and the crucifixion dance troubled her for opposing reasons. One was so selfish, the other so selfless. One dance was so wicked and defiling, the other so pure and guileless. One tricked and brought about death, and the other brought about an escape from death and brought life. The Lord had allowed Abia to witness both dances. *Why? Why? Why?* Her thoughts were consumed with searching for the answer.

While Abia sought answers, a great sadness and fear filled the hearts of the believers. Some were taking action. Joseph of Arimathea, a secret disciple of Jesus, had asked Pilate for Jesus' body. He had great respect for Jesus and did not want Jesus' body to stay on the cross for dogs and vultures to consume His remains. Mary, Jesus' mother, and some other women went in search of

Him to prepare Him for burial. Nicodemus, a converted Jewish leader, also came, bringing with him a mixture of myrrh and aloes of about 100 pounds in weight. They took Jesus' body to cleanse and anoint Him for burial. They bound Him in linen wrappings and laid Him in a tomb that had been hewn out of rock.

Sadness and fear filled the hearts of all believers. The Pharisees were afraid when they remembered what Jesus had said about rising after three days, and they complained to Pilate. He gave orders for the tomb to be secured with military guards and for a stone to seal its entry.

Mary Magdalene and Mary, the mother of James, went back to the grave site. A great earthquake had occurred. An angel of the Lord descended from Heaven and came and rolled away the stone and sat upon it. The appearance of the angel was like lightning, and his clothing was as white as snow. The guards shook with fear and became like dead men. The angel said to the women, "Do not be afraid; for I know that you are looking for Jesus who has been crucified. He is not here, for He has risen, just as He said. Come, see the place where He was lying. Go quickly and tell His disciples that He has risen from the dead; and behold, He is going ahead of you into Galilee, there you will see Him; behold, I have told you," the angel concluded.

When the two women arrived where the apostles were staying, the men were mourning and weeping over the death of Jesus. Mary Magdalene announced with great excitement that He was indeed alive and that she had seen Jesus in the garden near the tomb. She had actually taken hold of His feet and worshiped Him. But the apostles thought she was talking nonsense and would not believe her.

All doubts and fears were diminished when Jesus presented Himself alive to them many different times over a period of 40 days. He appeared to Peter in Jerusalem. Two travelers on the road saw Him. Behind a closed door Jesus appeared to ten disciples and

Thomas. Seven disciples saw Him while they fished. He spoke to 11 of His disciples and gave the "Great Commission." Five hundred brethren at one time saw Him as well.

As Jesus gathered together with His followers, they shared meals. Jesus told them many things about the Kingdom of God. He instructed them to return to Jerusalem, where they were to wait for what the Father had promised. John had baptized them in water, and they would soon be baptized by the Holy Spirit. He explained how it was necessary for Him to leave them and return to His Father. When He did, the Holy Spirit could come and be with them to make witnesses and disciples of them. He would baptize them in the name of the Father, Son, and Holy Spirit, and teach the Kingdom of God through them throughout the land.

With those things said, Jesus disappeared in a cloud. Everyone who was there stood staring into the empty sky when two men in white robes appeared. To the disciples they said, "Men of Galilee, why do you stand looking into the sky? This Jesus, who has been taken up from you into Heaven, will come in just the same way as you have watched Him go into Heaven."

The trip back to Jerusalem was a little over half a mile. The 11 returned and went to the upper room they had been using as a meeting place. Jesus' mother, Mary, His brothers, and many others, including Abia, Samuel and Mary, Judith and Abraham, and Yaron and Hannah—about 120 in all—met in this upper room for prayer. They praised and worshiped God and were in perfect unity, waiting as Jesus had instructed.

While they waited in the upper room, the disciples chose another to replace Judas, who had betrayed Jesus and had killed himself. Matthias was chosen by casting of lots.

Abia had not danced since Jesus rode into Jerusalem on the back of a donkey. She seemed to be in mourning. She had tried many times, but somehow the memory of Salome's dance and

later Jesus' death dance seeped into her mind, causing her to wonder why she had witnessed these dances. She knew in her heart
that there was a divine reason and that a day would come when it
would be time for her to dance again.

CHAPTER 26

The Prophetic Sound of the Fire

Jesus was crucified at the time of Passover. For 40 days Jesus appeared to people, and then He ascended into Heaven. Ten days later, many found safety and solace in the upper room, the same room where Jesus had shared what was now being called "the Last Supper" with the disciples. Many people were still in Jerusalem, having celebrated Passover there.

Just as King David had in days long gone, the ones gathered together to pray in the upper room stirred themselves in remembrance of God and His great deeds. The Torah was being spoken from the mouths of the oldest to the youngest as if it was a love story from God to humankind. They began to realize that ancient prophecies were being fulfilled in their lifetime. Jesus had come just as had been spoken by the prophets of old. He had died, was buried, came back to life, and was now sitting with God the Father in Heaven. Their minds were limited and could not begin to contain the magnitude of it all, but they were in awe of God. Everyone dropped to their knees, totally surrendered to the Lord Most High.

"One hundred twenty, one hundred twenty," Yaron repeated the number to himself after counting the number of people who had gathered in the upper room. At once he remembered the ancient chronicles. Aloud Yaron began to retell the story of when Solomon had finished the Temple of the Lord and had summoned the elders of Israel to Jerusalem. The Levites brought the Ark of the Covenant into the inner sanctuary of the Temple, the Most Holy Place. All the Levites who were musicians—Asaph, Heman, Jeduthun, and their sons and relatives—stood on the east side of the altar dressed in fine linen and playing cymbals, harps, and lyres. They were accompanied by 120 priests who sounded trumpets. The trumpeters and singers joined together in unity. With one voice they began to praise and thank God. They sang, "He is good; His love endures forever." Then the Temple of the Lord was filled with a cloud, for the glory of the Lord filled the Temple of God.

"Let us sing of the Lord and His goodness. Let us be trumpeters and singers who usher in the presence of God," Yaron's voice pleaded in excitement and joy.

Suddenly, Abia could hold back no longer. She had to dance. Having expressed by mouth every word of worship and praise she knew, there seemed to be no other way to continue to express her love, adoration, and devotion to God than to dance. Ever so slowly, she began to rise from the floor. Her feet, arms, and body became fluid like warm honey that moved to a rhythm put inside her from the day of her conception in her mother's womb by the hands of God Himself. With surrendered body, will, spirit, and mind, Abia danced before the Lord.

The joy that rose within her caused her to spin around and around in abandonment. With wild excitement, Abia danced to celebrate Him and what He meant to her. When Abia remembered that she had not been able to dance for so many years and how He miraculously had healed her, she danced in wonder and awe of Him. She danced because she could.

All the men and women in the room were caught in the rain of worship as joy and celebration became contagious. Gradually, Abia became aware that others had joined their little band of 120. Who were these people? Bewildered, she strained her eyes to try to recognize the great crowd that had gathered with them in the upper room.

All at once, the men cried as if with one loud voice, "They are the Great Cloud of Witnesses from past generations." It was incredible. The prophets of old were allowed to gather together with new believers of this day. The Great Cloud of Witnesses, who had prophesied this day, were rewarded and allowed to share the celebration of God being united once again with His people. It was as if all inhabitants of Heaven—saints and angels, Father and Son—were caught up into the excitement and jubilation and were dancing with them. Abia saw one whom she believed to be Miriam with a tambourine in her hand accompanied by a large company of dancers. King David, the dancing king, led the way.

Without warning, a sudden gale-force wind rushed in, sounding as if it was coming from Heaven. It too danced around the room. A fresh, heavenly fragrance was unleashed to fill the room. The vibrant colors that accompanied the wind were ones never seen on Earth before. As the wind blew the colors, they transformed into brand-new colors never before seen in this realm. Like an unrestrained wildfire, the wind swirled around them.

Rays of gold and white lights appeared as God's glory came rushing in from Heaven. A giant cylinder of light formed from the ceiling and settled in the center of the room. The rays of golden and white lights quivered with excitement as the glory of God entered and was followed by the seven spirits of God: the Spirit of the Lord, the Spirit of Wisdom, the Spirit of Understanding, the Spirit of Counsel, the Spirit of Power, the Spirit of Knowledge, and the Spirit of the Fear of the Lord. These spirits were separate, but one.

Around and around they went spinning into an apex at the center of the room. In a wondrous and glorious explosion, the Holy Spirit of God was discharged into flames of fire. Flaming fire darted back and forth around the room until a holy visitation was made to each of those who were gathered. Heaven was kissing Earth as a flame kissed each head.

The Holy Spirit poured into them, filling them like a pitcher pours forth wine into a cup. Bypassing natural boundaries of the rim, the Holy Spirit poured into each cup the very presence of God and the very power of God. Love, joy, peace, patience, kindness, goodness, faithfulness, gentleness, and self-control entered and overflowed from them until the contents of each cup touched its neighbors. The wine flowed with the virtues of Jesus. The pouring and spilling out was a continuous movement. The whole floor became saturated with wine, causing it to flow outward toward the doorway of the upper room and eventually to stairs that led to the city streets.

From the center of the room came another blast of light as two angelic beings brought forth a golden box that would be envied by any earthly king.

"But the one who joins himself to the Lord is one spirit with Him and is charged with representing Him on Earth. Speak, know, and act like Jesus. A variety of gifts for ministry and for the common good are presented to you!" exclaimed the beings as they opened the gifts of the Holy Spirit. Verbal gifts of prophecy, tongues, and interpretation of tongues arose from the golden box and were poured out upon each of them. Knowing gifts of wisdom, knowledge, and discerning of spirits came forth and were imparted into them. Doing or action gifts of miracles, faith, and healing were transferred into their newly awakened spirits.

God the Father's long awaited dream of inhabiting His people once again was being realized because of His Son, Jesus. People were meant to house God just as Moses' tabernacle and other temples demonstrated in the natural. He wants His people filled with His knowledge and understanding, but more importantly, with His presence. Astoundingly, the believers had become the temple of the Holy Spirit.

To their further amazement, each began to speak in a different language or tongue as the Holy Spirit prompted. No one was taught the language by natural means of learning, but was enabled to speak by a supernatural means of the Holy Spirit.

It was then that Abia heard the new sound. It was different than the wind sound, yet it came from within. It was a sound within the sound. It was an ancient sound; it was the sound before there was sound. Abia had never heard this sound before, yet it was somehow familiar to her newly awakened spirit. She knew it was a heavenly sound because she could not find its match within her own understanding and experience. Abia's spirit, soul, and body were somehow made aware of this new and rhythmic reverberation. Intuitively, Abia knew it as the prophetic sound of the dance.

As Abia heard the sound, she was given discernment as to what the sound of the dance meant. The Holy Spirit would unite with dance in a divine form of worship because God could now completely inhabit the praises of His people. This dance would be received from God by the Holy Spirit and manifested through movement to bring forth a message. This was to be a new and glorious form of communication from the Father, through the Son, by the Holy Spirit, to speak to His people. This dance required the infilling of the Holy Spirit to hear His voice and the power to obey His commands. The movements given to the dancer were the actual movements of God in the Spirit realm. The movements would be released from Heaven by the Holy Spirit and received here on Earth to accomplish His purposes and desires. All authority in Heaven and on Earth would be given to prophesy and give testimony of Jesus and to execute on Earth what was being said in Heaven.

The enemies of God would not be able to understand this nonverbal method of prayer, intercession, and warfare. This was to be a prophetic dance. It would be an incredible tool for worship and a weapon of war against God's enemies. It would bring confusion to the camps of the enemy, while bringing peace and comfort to the hearts of His people. Holy dancers would ascend to high places of worship and reach depths unattainable until now. The Holy dancers would descend to carry out the messages through divine movements. The dances would speak the oracles of God from ancient paths to bring about changes now and for the future.

Prophetic dance would follow Jesus' example. He patterned Himself by the Father, speaking only what He heard the Father speak and doing only what He saw the Father do. A prophetic dancer would speak through movement only that which Jesus would speak and do. This dance would be authentic, holy, and purified by the leading of the Holy Spirit and allowed only through the filter of love.

God was restoring humankind to Himself. Dance would be a visual demonstration of the Word of God, the heart of God, and the love of God. It would make evident the new habitation of His Presence within the temple of earthly vessels. By divine guidance, a dancer in complete unity with the will of God would cause and bring about earthly changes. The spiritual could invade the physical realm to bring about healing, peace, restoration, refreshing, deliverance, repair, renewal, and everything else Jesus accomplished on the cross and with His authority.

Abia recognized that called, anointed holy prophetic dancers would minister God's love to others one day. Their prayer language through dance movements would enable them to come boldly before the throne of God and request that the enemy's camp be plundered and that everything that had been stolen, killed, or destroyed would be restored.

Abia's spirit drank greedily from the wealth of knowledge and revelation the Holy Spirit was imparting, but her mind could not fathom all its meaning. She needed the wisdom to accompany the knowledge. Abia was discovering that very spirit was an unlimited container to hold spiritual things while her flesh was restricted and inadequate. Abia was still trying to figure out how she could be in the presence of God and yet still be alive!

How Abia ended up in a heap, face down on the floor of the upper room, she had no recollection. All she knew was that when the presence of God, in the form of the Holy Spirit, entered the room, she could not abase herself enough. Her body, mind, and spirit responded without hesitation to the glory, authority, and majesty of the Lord. It was as if she had been asleep, but was now awakened and vibrantly alive as never before. It would take a lifetime to soak in what had been shown to her, but she now had a Teacher, Helper, and Counselor.

A whisper got her attention while her ears, mind, heart, and spirit strained to hear His voice. "Abia," He said. God had spoken her name! She had heard that voice before. It was Jesus' voice, and it was the same as when He called Abia His dancer three years prior.

Abia's mind was reeling from the wonder of it all. This voice was not one she heard from her natural ears, but it came from within the pulsing spirit now alive within her.

"Abia," the Holy Spirit's voice spoke again as if to give her practice hearing from her spirit and not her ears. "You are a holy dancer called to minister on Earth as it is in Heaven. Have you heard the sound of a new dance?"

"Yes, my Lord" the automatic response came from Abia's lips, acknowledging and answering the call all in the same instance.

"Your dance will be more than thanksgiving and expressions of joy, as you have been made aware. It will invite the presence of God. It will be more than the physical or outward expression of the inward relationship you have had with Me. From this precise moment, you will dance in spirit and in truth. The truth imparted to you today will not be lost to you and will be revealed in the days ahead. Today, you have been given My Spirit within you. What truth do you wish to know?"

The questions that entered her thoughts were ones that had restlessly and impatiently circled her mind for many months now. Abia's response was automatic, "Why did I witness Salome's dance and Jesus' death dance?" She voiced her response in humility.

The Holy Spirit spoke to Abia's spirit with the following reply, "The first dance will be last, and the last dance will be first." As if sensing her thoughts before there was time to utter them, the Holy Spirit explained. "The last dance of Jesus' death is all-important and essential. Everything is to be centered on the finished work of the cross. Reflect on Salome's counterfeit dance, and I'll reveal more truth."

A new and wonderful peace flooded Abia's spirit, a peace she had not known until then. God was speaking to humankind without a mediator, such as a king, priest, or prophet, and He had spoken directly to her! Abia's spirit, body, and mind were whirling like the convergence of massive hurricanes. Abia had not sensed Him exiting the room, for indeed, He would never leave again.

A great crowd had gathered outside when they heard the tremendous thunderous sound from within the walls of the upper room. Devout people from every nation who had gathered in Jerusalem for Pentecost were drawn by the sound. Upon arriving, they heard their own languages being spoken, testifying to the mighty deeds of God. They wondered what God was doing in their midst and what it all meant.

Some people, however, mocked the devout and all the people who had gathered in the upper room, saying that they must be intoxicated. Criticism flowed from the scoffers' sober hearts—those who disapproved anything they did not understand.

Despite the scorners, the once unstable leader, Peter, stood with the 11 disciples to dispute the lie that they were drunk on sweet wine. New wine had been given to them by the Holy Spirit, which was immediately seen by Peter's boldness as he preached to the highly religious crowd that had gathered. Gone was all self-confidence, having been replaced with confidence that came from the Holy Spirit. Peter was empowered by the Holy Spirit to speak and teach despite his own personal sins and mistakes, giving proof of God's forgiveness and redemption.

With an audience comprised of people from the whole world— men, women, slaves, Jews, and Gentiles—the Holy Spirit empowered Peter to rightly discern ancient prophecies to the people. He proved by the Holy Scriptures that everything that had happened to Jesus was planned by God and that no government or religious officials could alter or control it. Jesus' resurrection was the proof and ultimate sign that all Jesus said was true.

Peter and his message were Spirit-filled, and those who heard him were pricked in their hearts and immediately convicted of their sins. Having personally experienced salvation, Peter could then lead them into a relationship with their Savior. "Repent, and each of you be baptized in the name of Jesus Christ for the forgiveness of your sins; and you will receive the gift of the Holy Spirit," he instructed.

Peter's first sermon added 3,000 souls in one day to the growing number of believers in Jesus. Devoting themselves to the apostles and their teachings, many gathered to pray and were united in fellowship with each other. In memory of Jesus and in remembrance of His teachings, they broke bread together just as Jesus had done with His disciples in the upper room. Everyone was filled with awe and wonder as they remembered all that Jesus taught and spoke of, but they were equally amazed by the many signs and wonders that were taking place through the apostles.

Everyone was wild with excitement, and yet there was an element of the unknown that caused an unsettling within each of them. They had dual identities for the first time in history—Jews and believers in Jesus. Armed with the Comforter and Holy Helper, the infant Church began to grow and mature. One thing was extrememly evident; life was never to be the same.

CHAPTER 27

The Virgin Shall Rejoice in the Dance

Jesus' death and resurrection had changed the lives of all who believed in Him. Unfortunately, they lived in their own land, but because of their new beliefs, they were treated as aliens. Life for the new believers was getting more difficult with each passing day. The Jewish Sanhedrin hated the followers of Jesus because of the rising numbers of people who were leaving the traditions of the Jews in favor of the newly found freedom in Christ. And that meant they did not have as many people to swindle money from. The Sanhedrin, to maintain order, became less tolerant of believing Jews. Many believers resented their fellow Jews and began to assign blame for Jesus' death on the Sanhedrin and the crowds of people who wanted Him crucified.

Jesus was a Jew, but the ruling authorities framed Him in order to get rid of Him. Jesus' rise in popularity was considered a threat to them. The corrupt Jewish government became angry because the people, after hearing Jesus' teachings, were less tolerant of them. The people finally had an authentic leader in Jesus to judge others by, and many of the high priests and other religious leaders did not like how they fared. When the Jewish government leaders made attempts to quiet the so-called rumors of Jesus' resurrection by killing anyone who made reference to it, the Jewish believers in Jesus tried to fight back in any way they could. As a result, they were being imprisoned, beaten, and harassed daily.

Other believers blamed the Roman government for not stopping the death sentencing when there was insufficient evidence to have Jesus crucified. It was known far and wide that the Romans took bribes for protection of the high priests of the Jews leaving no protection for believers of Jesus. The Roman government started putting unreasonable demands on belivers of Jesus. They forced them to meet in the city's catacombs, sewers, and dark alleys because they were not allowed to gather publicly. Rome was hoping to stop the spread of the new religion, blaming it for the civil unrest. So the conditions and treatment for believers declined rapidly.

The Romans thought the new believers in Jesus were strange. In the practice of taking communion, Romans believed Jesus' followers drank real blood and ate real human flesh, not having any knowledge of the symbolic practice. They believed they practiced some type of cannibalism and thought the group was highly superstitious. They had heard rumors that followers of Jesus thought of themselves as powerful, and the Romans grew highly suspicious and watchful of them. The believers did not participate in Roman public festivals, avoided joining their military, and rejected many Roman traditions. Romans grew resentful of the believers who did not gamble or practice the sexual immorality that was widespread. The Roman people were a prideful people and felt rebuffed when the believing Jews voiced any criticism of their pagan practices.

The Romans were not devoutly religious, but did believe their Caesar to be their god, and they had other gods as well. Roman rule demanded control. If Caesar was to be worshiped, then everyone had to worship him. They offered wine and incense to the other gods, who they believed had special powers over everyday matters, such as crop growing, military might, and rainmaking. High prices of punishment came as a result of not following the sacred customs of the Romans. Rome had the belief that bad things happened in society if the gods were not properly respected or worshiped. Because of the civil unrest between the Jews and due to the fact the Jews would not worship their gods, Rome kept a tight rein on them and believed they were bad for society.

In the months following Pentecost, murders of Christians, as Rome was calling them, were being reported daily. The deaths of these martyrs seemed to have an opposite reaction to what was expected by the unbelievers and government. The Church grew and grew. People were receiving Jesus as their personal Savior and were being filled with the Holy Spirit to serve and to do the greater things that Jesus had spoken about.

As often as possible, believers in Jesus gathered together to pray for individual needs, for the apostles, and for the Kingdom of God to be spread far and wide. It was such an exciting time to gather with the others, but never were they without fear of being discovered by the Roman armies.

It had always been a specific practice of the Jews to gather and worship God both privately and publicly. This had been tolerated and accepted by the Romans, but it had become more and more dangerous. Any formal gathering was viewed as a possible rebellion, so they were watched continually. The group of soldiers assigned to the Ben-David neighborhood was tolerant, but it was known with whom their allegiance lay. The soldiers were aware of the fact that the threat of death was hanging over each soldier's head for disobedience, so there was no choice for them but to do their duty.

Uncertainty seemed to be a familiar blanket, one that had covered the Jewish people since the beginning of time. They had learned to stand up in times of uncertainty and in adversity. So, as with those from generations past, many gathered to remember and worship God, who was always found faithful.

Jewish history is littered with wars against the Jews, social injustices, and misconduct toward the people of God by her fiercest enemies. The Jews desired justice and felt restoration was needed in every part of society from its corruption. They yearned for restitution of the former glory when the nation of Israel was called the apple of God's eye. These were changes only God could do, but many believed that following the former religious ways would be enough to bring this about.

The Levites and priests had long ago made sacrifices of worship as worship leaders. All the people benefited from their sacrifices, but they did not, or could not, enter into that holy place themselves. As people reflected on the events of Pentecost, they wondered, *Could what was experienced on the day of Pentecost mean that every member of every believing household could have the same anointing for serving and worshiping God previously available to only Levites or priests?*

This was incredible news for some, but others were consumed with jealousy because they did not want their position or power to be shared with anyone. Some decided to leave the teachings of Jesus and join the Jews, who practiced the old, familiar ways.

When the enemy comes, a united front always works best in protecting against an attack; but what happens if there is no united front and the enemy is within? Many Christians were Jews, but the religious leaders were excluding them from participating with the other Jews in time-honored traditional practices such as worshiping in the Temple or synagogues. Christian Jews were persecuted for their belief in Jesus, but so were others. The Jewish leadership made the decisions to prohibit those who believed in Jesus—Jew or Gentile—from entering the Temple or synagogues.

While gathering in homes to worship had been long practiced by the Jews, it became a necessity when many were excommunicated from the synagogues. During the gatherings, the power of God would rise in the hearts and spirits of the believers and inspire the people to worship the Lord and to share their personal testimonies with others. Rich and poor alike shared from their hearts how Jesus had rescued them from some form of darkness and had brought them into His marvelous light. Incredible stories of how Jesus had touched, healed, and changed their lives stirred hope within the hearts of all.

The harmonious sounds of voices that had weathered many trials, tribulations, and persecutions made a passionate serenade to Jesus. The ancient words of the prophet Jeremiah were put to music and sung, bringing comfort to all.

> *Hear the word of the Lord, O nations,*
> *And declare in the coastlands afar off,*
> *And say, "He who scattered Israel will gather him*
> *And keep him as a shepherd keeps his flock."*
> *...Then the virgin will rejoice in the dance,*
> *And the young men and the old, together,*
> *For I will turn their mourning into joy*
> *And will comfort them and give them joy for their sorrow.*

It seemed everyone was in deep reflection about their faith and the trustworthiness of God. The song stirred a longing within the hearts of the most aged and young alike.

Suddenly, there was an urgency to remember everything Jesus had said and done while He was with the people. Everyone began to realize, by the insightful power of the Holy Spirit, that they had been warned of the events of His death before they occurred. Jesus had also said what would happen to those who followed Him when He was back at the right hand of the Father in Heaven. Each description of events from Jesus' short life was confirming the ancient prophecies. From Jesus' foretold birth and predicted crucifixion, to His long-awaited ascension, history was being made and woven together as one would carefully weave a tapestry.

It was incredible how the chronicle of Jesus' life brought about such hope of His Kingdom being on Earth and yet, at the same time, so such uncertainty. No one knew what the day ahead would bring. Fear and anxiety filled even the hearts of the most aged of men at times. Doubt and unbelief partnered to make even the most faithful falter. Many had expected a king who would destroy the evil ones on Earth, but the Kingdom Jesus spoke of was not of this Earth. What would become of the people? Only God knew for certain.

John, son of Zebedee and the brother of James, spoke to the hearts of all who were gathered one day as he remembered the following words of Jesus.

"But now I am going to Him who sent Me; and none of you asks Me, 'Where are You going?' But because I have said these things to you, sorrow has filled your heart. But I tell you the truth, it is to your advantage that I go away; for if I do not go away, the Helper will not come to you; but if I go, I will send Him to you. And He, when He comes, will convict the world concerning sin and righteousness and judgment; concerning sin, because they do not believe Me; and concerning righteousness, because I go to the Father and you no longer see Me; and concerning judgment, because the ruler of this world has been judged.

"I have many more things to say to you, but you cannot bear them now. But when He, the Spirit of truth, comes, He will guide you into all the truth; for He will not speak on His own initiative, but whatever He hears, He will speak; and He will disclose to you what is to come. He will glorify Me, for He will take of Mine and will disclose it to you. All things that the Father has are Mine. Therefore, I said that He takes of Mine and will disclose it to you.

"These things I have spoken to you, so that in Me you may have peace. In the world you have tribulation, but take courage; I have overcome the world."

With those words, everyone began to rejoice and worship the Lord Most High. Believing in Jesus and what He said was the difference between life and death. Their lives, long or short, were to be lived as Jesus lived His. They were not left as orphans; the Holy Spirit was with all believers in Jesus, not just with the high priests and appointed kings as in days long ago. No matter what life was to bring, God the Father, God the Son, and now God the Holy Spirit were with them for the first time in history. His mercy and grace astounded everyone who had gathered to worship God that day.

Some ached for the former way of life, while others had mixed feelings about the past and an excitement for the future. There seemed to be an expectancy of new worship since the atoning death of the Lamb of God and the infilling of the Holy Spirit. In many ways, it seemed as though it was the worst of times, while at the same time, could one dare hope that better days were ahead?

CHAPTER 28

Slow Dancing

"I have many more things to say to you, but you cannot bear them now," resounded though Abia's spirit as they walked home from the gathering that evening.

"What things do You want to say to me, Lord? Why can I not bear them now?"

The silence that followed gave her a sense that more was to come. She yearned to be alone with Him, to dance with Him. She yearned to hear His voice again and the incredible things He had promised to tell her.

Abia's calling had always seemed to be one involving dance, although she had not realized it was a calling until now. Finally she began to understand why she never stopped thinking about dancing, even when she was unable to walk. When Abia prayed, she danced. When she worshiped, she danced. She sought the Lord time after time to try to piece together what He was teaching her about this new dance that came from the sound given by the Holy Spirit.

The Holy Spirit of God had told her that Jesus' death dance was pivotal. He had also said she was to review the counterfeit dance of Salome for more revelation. It seemed that He had created a new pattern or model to which dance was to be remolded and conformed.

Abia felt as if she could hear the voice of the prophet Jeremiah quoting God to this new generation of dancers everywhere:

I have loved you with an everlasting love;
Therefore I have drawn you with lovingkindness.
Again I will build you and you will be rebuilt,
O virgin of Israel!
Again you will take up your tambourines,
And go forth to the dances of the merrymakers.
…Then the virgin will rejoice in the dance,
And the young men and the old, together,
For I will turn their mourning into joy
And will comfort them and give them joy for their sorrow.

As wonderful as it was to gather with other believers, Abia desired the intimacy that had begun to develop since Pentecost when she danced alone with the Holy Spirit of God. Dancing seemed to be a portal to His presence. It was an entrance way by which she could gain access and could approach Him. Her spirit could unite with His in a cherished way. It was as if Abia knew that, if she could worship Him in the dance, He would bring revelation to her spirit.

Once more, the old and new questions surfaced. Why had she witnessed the dance that led to John the Baptist's death and the crucifixion dance of Jesus? The Holy Spirit's advice to focus on the counterfeit to discover the original arose from her spirit. Again, just like the questions that swirled in her mind, the Spirit led Abia to dance for revelation.

Physically Abia danced, but she also danced with the Spirit. The incredible language of tongues that was imparted to her when baptized by the Holy Spirit became the music she danced to. Faith was growing and so was her love for the One who had saved her soul.

Worship became richer and more intentional as she learned to lean on the Holy Spirit. Abia did not fully know what she said to Him as she used the new language, but she knew enough to know when she was worshiping Him because the sound of her voice and heart became full of admiration and joy. After a while she began to tell the difference when He spoke to her. When the Holy Spirit spoke words of encouragement to her, faith grew and His peace flooded the soul and spirit, quieting her mind from doubt and fear.

Instructional words like swirl, turn, hop, spring about, raise your arms, look up, kneel, jump, and clap—to name only a few— were some she heard Him speak. When she was obedient and did as He instructed, Abia was rewarded with another word or phrase. When she did not hear anything, she knew it was acceptable for her to move in the dance any way she desired, just like a child who, without thought, skips to reach for her father's arms.

Abia's prayer language was one He understood, and He brought understanding to her as well. The exchange of words of knowledge and discernment allowed by the Holy Spirit helped her to know Him and the ways He wanted her to dance before Him.

The Holy Spirit was teaching Abia to dance with Him. He moved and she followed. When Abia led with praise and worship, He followed by steering her mind, body, and spirit to new thoughts, new movements, and new revelation. The new revelation brought new movements and new thoughts of Him, which led her back to worshiping and praising Him. The dance exchange was exhilarating!

Once when Abia was dancing and thanking Him for being wise and powerful beyond all else, she heard Him speak into her own thoughts the phrase, "Humbly bow and arise in the power of My strength."

Without hesitation and in full obedience, Abia lifted her arms Heavenward and lowered them in a dramatic sweep downward, bowing from the waist. As she did, love filled her heart in a manner she had never before felt. The love for Him intensified, as did new revelation of the love He had for her, but amazingly it did not stop there. Abia sensed a new awareness of the love He had for others as well. The realization of His love for humankind caused her to love them as well. Armed with love, Abia arose from the bow with the joy of the Lord flooding her heart and spirit as she spun around and around in the strength of His love.

Eagerly Abia anticipated any and all opportunities to dance with Him and hear Jesus' voice speak to her through the power of the Holy Spirit. She lived to worship God, and it was in worship that Abia felt the most alive.

Many times she gathered with other believers and danced in a corporate setting, which was wonderful. At other times, Abia looked forward to coming home to make herself ready to dance as if she were anticipating a gentleman caller!

CHAPTER 29

Dancing With
Eyes Wide Open

Fires were being lit as the daylight was dimming. The smell of firewood and prepared food permeated the air. Christians, as they were beginning to be called, were gathering to share meals and exchange stories of the day's events in common courtyards throughout the city of Jerusalem.

As night fell, family and friends assembled at various homes to sing, dance, and worship God. After the evening meal, Samuel and Mary joined his parents and Abia as they sat outside the kitchen room in the common courtyard. It was late fall, and the night temperatures would soon make everyone move back inside their homes to escape the cold. Having just celebrated the Feast of Trumpets or Rosh Hashanah, the beginning of the Jewish New Year in late September, this night was unusually warm for the beginning of October.

Samuel and Mary had married in late summer, so they were still considered newlyweds. Like all newlyweds, they kept to themselves and away from anything that would distract them from each other. From the way Samuel looked at Mary, it was evident he had indeed married the love of his life. To have Abia's best friend, Mary, as part of the family was glorious. She missed Judith sorely since she and Abraham had married, but Mary was now part of the family, and she could not have been more thrilled.

Mary had been her best friend ever since her earliest memory. Her visits, when she was crippled from the accident, were always filled with the latest news, and as children they loved to brush each other's long brown hair. Abia taught Mary to sew, and she taught Abia how to make baskets from straw.

Mary remembered that her father had made for Samuel a new shofar or trumpet. He had asked if it was possible for Samuel to visit her father's house to pick it up after the evening meal. So Samuel departed to retrieve the shofar.

As the night grew darker, the sound of music from the neighboring homes within the confines of the courtyard grew louder. Gone were the days when only men could give praise because the priest legalistically forbade men and women from singing together, considering it too promiscuous. Even songs were beginning to change from a focus that was just on God to one that included Jesus.

People began to sing songs created by the leading of the Holy Spirit. As the Spirit of the Lord began to move in Abia's heart, she began to dance. Abia began to dance and worship to the sound of new, inspired songs played with instruments that created new sounds straight from Heaven. It was the most amazing sound they had ever heard. They were worshiping their God, Jesus, and the Holy Spirit without ritual, but with love and relationship with Him. The sound was pure and holy.

Just then, Abia began to sing with the heavenly language of tongues she had received at Pentecost. Her body spun around and around, causing her dress to make a huge circle around her while she lifted her hands in surrendered abandonment. Suddenly, she saw a vision. It was a vision of Samuel seen through the eyes of her spirit by the empowerment of the Holy Spirit. He was walking back home from Mary's father's house with the shofar gift in his hand. He had decided to take a shortcut down a dimly lit street, and in the Spirit, Abia saw danger approach him. In the shadows, two Roman soldiers were running to apprehend him. Abia's heart was beating as fast as a drum. "Jesus, help him!" she cried, but did not stop dancing.

With each prayer that poured forth from her mouth came a matching movement to her dance. When she prayed for protection, the Holy Spirit revealed a dance movement to her mind, which was to bring the edge of her skirt up with her two hands as if it was a blanket to comfort and shield them. As she proclaimed Jesus as Samuel's strong tower to run into in times of trouble, the movement He gave to Abia was similar to the one she had seen Jesus do when He was being crucified and did His death dance. He spread His arms apart on that terrible day at the cross of Calvary to welcome all who would believe in Him. Abia lifted both arms out to her side to imitate Him.

The words of King David came to her mind: *"In my distress I called upon the Lord, yes, I cried to my God; and from His temple He heard my voice, and my cry for help came into His ears."*

Then in her spirit Abia heard the roar of a mighty lion and saw the soldiers turn and run from sight. Shaking from head to toe, Abia finally collapsed on the floor in a heap as her intercession dance came to an end.

Just then, Samuel ran into the courtyard running as fast as his legs could carry him. His face was pale with fright. Abia joined him just as he began to tell his story—after he had caught his breath and drank the water Mary brought for him.

While on his way home from retrieving the shofar from Mary's father's house, he had decided to take a shortcut. He was blowing the new shofar rather loudly when suddenly he heard from behind soldiers' footsteps rapidly approaching him.

When he started to run, he tripped and got entangled in a muslin blanket that was hung on a clothesline to dry. This forced him to hide himself in a deep, shadow-covered alcove of one of the buildings. To escape, he quickly planned to turn in the opposite direction and run as fast as he could. Samuel did not know what other dangers might befall him if he ran, but felt there was nothing else to do.

Still crouched in the shadows of the buildings, he was about to make his break and run when heavy footsteps and clanging swords against the belts of the soldiers made him change his mind. Samuel held his breath in fear, not knowing whether or not they had seen him. Louder and louder came the approaching soldiers hurrying toward him.

Frozen by fear, he shut his eyes and waited for the soldiers to capture him within the next few seconds. The Roman soldiers halted just five feet from Samuel, who was still hidden from sight by the shadows of the night.

With a quick prayer and passing thoughts of regret for not being able to live out his life with Mary and to experience being a parent, he waited to die. But, nothing happened. He opened his eyes when he discovered the footsteps had stopped, and he had not been revealed. Still in danger, he waited.

Suddenly and without warning, the Roman soldiers pivoted and started to run away from Samuel in the opposite direction from which they had come. Something seemed to startle the two soldiers; panic seemed to grip them, and they began to run. As they ran away, the soldiers kept peering over their shoulders in Samuel's direction, as if something or someone were after them.

Samuel decided to stay in the safety of the alcove for a little while longer, making sure the soldiers would not return before he revealed himself from his safe hiding spot. Some shake at the first signs of trouble, and others do not shake until the trouble is over; the latter was the case for Samuel. He shook from a mixture of fear and relief. With a trembling voice He offered to God a quick, but heartfelt prayer of thanksgiving to God for His divine protection, no matter how puzzling it seemed.

What made the soldiers do an about-face and run? What had they seen to cause them to run wildly away, all the while looking over their shoulders as if something were after them?

As Samuel looked down the street into the darkness and got ready to stand and leave his hiding place, he suddenly saw something move in the shadows directly behind him. His eyes were locked on to the movement in the shadows. He strained his eyes, trying to discover the identity of the mysterious shadow. Whatever it was, it had made two highly trained Roman soldiers run for cover. Whatever was lurking in the gloom of the dimly lit street that threatened the two soldiers was about to show itself to him as well.

As he relayed the story to the family, everyone was eagerly awaiting its conclusion. Mary had stationed herself under his arm in a perpetual hug to reassure herself he was indeed well. Without warning, Samuel unexpectedly backed away from Mary as he began to remove the outer tunic he had been wearing.

"Samuel Ben-David!" Mary began to scold him. "With your whole family and all your neighbors listening intently, there is no need for you to attempt to make it any more dramatic than it already is!" she said with a voice that trembled from hearing how close she had come to losing her husband. She also felt a little miffed by the little shove he had given her when he was trying to take off his tunic.

With a sideways grin that he always had when he was up to mischief, he finally reached into his outer shirt and gently brought a long-haired, golden-colored kitten out from beneath its material. The kitten greeted the family with a sweet "meow" as Samuel said, "This, my family, friends, and dear wife, gave me quite a fright tonight!"

Everyone's frightened glances softened in surprise as the small kitten emerged from the warmth of Samuel's shirt. The nervous tension in the room seemed to vanish as it gave way to laughter. Mary, as she realized the reason for Samuel's little push, joined in the laughter with the rest.

All at once, revelation came to Abia! She started jumping up and down and spinning her brother, Samuel, around and around by the arm in her excitement.

"OK, OK, OK, Abia," Samuel chiding Abia as his tolerance for his sister soon became annoyance, just as it sometimes had when she was younger.

"Listen to me everyone," Abia pleaded with excitement. "I will tell you of yet another story of the goodness of our Father in Heaven, our Savior Jesus, and the Holy Spirit," she continued.

Abia explained how she was given the revelation of what had just happened when she was dancing. It spilled forth from her spirit as she recounted the events of her vision to the family and the alarmed friends who had gathered to find out why Samuel was running so fast in the dark.

This dance was like no other. It was something that she never knew could happen while she danced, and she was eager to share her experience with the others.

"It began when I was dancing and worshiping God," Abia explained. "While I was dancing, I saw a vision of Samuel, and I somehow knew he was in trouble. While I was praying in the new heavenly language I received at Pentecost, the Spirit of the Living God gave me certain dance moves that matched the prayers I prayed. He allowed me to participate as the vision unfolded. The prayers and dance moves seemed automatic, as if they were guided by the Holy Spirit," she said with her voice full of amazement.

"My prayer of intercession for divine help for Samuel was heard, but greater still was how I was given insight and discernment on how to pray for him based on the help from the Holy Spirit!" she exclaimed. Recollecting Samuel's story, Abia began to see more fully the meanings of the dance moves. She had lifted the edges of her skirt as if it were a blanket used for protection, comfort, and as a shield at the very moment Samuel became entangled by a blanket that was hung on the clothesline. The blanket caused him to hide instead of run away. If he had kept running, he would have most likely been caught by the soldiers.

As she recalled praying for Samuel to run into Jesus, who is a strong tower, the Holy Spirit had used her open arms while dancing to depict Jesus' arms of protection. Jesus' protection took the form of a dimly lit alcove of safety found between the arms of two adjoining buildings.

The Holy Spirit, by the gift of words of knowledge, had given her an ability to know the unknown and to pray specially against the dangers. The Holy Spirit had said that the Lord inhabits the praises of His people! Jesus was the answer to all prayer. She learned that it is better to pray the answer rather than the problem. When she did this, Samuel's way was made safe.

God was using the gift of tongues as a way to communicate His knowledge and wisdom to the human mind and human spirit through the power of the Holy Spirit. The Holy Spirit was allowing Abia to participate in a new type of prayer by acting out the movements that came from the revelations of the Spirit through dance. Yet, it seemed like more than just acting out the movements. There seemed to be power in the movements themselves. Dance movements communicated the needs on Earth and the answers that were found in Heaven. Dance was a new type of prayer and a tool for intercession and warfare.

As Abia explained all this, everyone was amazed and astonished at the goodness of God and the new ways He was using the dance.

Suddenly, Abia remembered leaving out an important piece of the story. She recalled, while she was dancing and praying, that a psalm from King David came to her mind. *"The Lord has heard the voice of my weeping. The Lord has heard my supplication, the Lord receives my prayer."* While praying as she danced, she remembered hearing, by spiritual ears, the sound of a massive lion's roar. The roar of the lion shook the ground with its loud sound, which caused the soldiers to run away to escape with their lives.

Yaron's laugh became infectious as he held the kitten in the air with both hands and repeated the remainder of the exact psalm of King David: *"The Lord has heard the voice of my weeping. The Lord has heard my supplication, the Lord receives my prayer. **All my enemies will be ashamed and greatly dismayed; they shall turn back, they will suddenly be ashamed.**"*

With a small kitten, God had confounded the mighty Roman soldiers, and they had retreated, totally bewildered. Yaron, still holding the tiny sleeping "lion," pronounced that their new pet's name should be Judah! One of the names of God is "Lion of Judah." As a reminder and in honor of the Lion of Judah's mighty roar that saved Samuel from possible death at the hands of the Roman soldiers, Judah took his place with the Ben-David family as its newest addition.

CHAPTER 30

Following the Sound of a New Partner

As Abia lay in her bed waiting for sleep that night, her mind and spirit again were whirling from the events of the day and evening. It was truly amazing that God would open the heavens for her to have His perspective and understanding. It was equally amazing that the Holy Spirit had allowed her to participate through the dance of intercession to bring about change in the life of Samuel. This seemed to be an example of what He had spoken in the upper room that day.

Revelation from Heaven came by the Holy Spirit to her spirit and was manifested into dance movements that brought forth change in the earthly realm. Jesus had said that those on Earth would have the ability to speak in His name by His authority inside the will of God. He said these same ones would have the keys of the Kingdom. These keys are to bind or forbid on Earth what is not allowed in Heaven. Jesus also said those with these keys possessed the same power to loose or permit on Earth that which is allowed in Heaven. In Heaven, there is protection from evil and harm. To pray for that on Earth for Samuel was within God's will. Therefore, it was loosed on Earth.

The dance as a means of prayer through the leading of the Holy Spirit brought the revelation and power to use the keys and change the Earth. The truth of it was almost more than could be comprehended. This one thing Abia knew for sure: It was an incredible honor to be called, equipped, and anointed to dance prophetically.

"I have many more things to say to you," said the now familiar voice of the Holy Spirit.

"Can I bear them now?" Abia asked.

"Yes," He said.

Abia's body, mind, and spirit jumped to attention as if she were a well-trained soldier awaiting orders from her superior.

The revelation and discernment that were to occur would be life-changing. He was bringing clarity and understanding to the things she had been given.

As she continued to lie in her bed, thoughts of sleep were gone. She pondered all the events that had occurred including John the Baptist's death, Jesus' death dance, the revelation sound of the dance given in the upper room, and now the dance that helped deliver Samuel away from harm. She left her bed and fell to the floor, holding her belly as if giving birth. In travail, the Holy Spirit was birthing more revelation in her spirit for the dance. This new and unique prophetic dance would require more than movements alone to bring about the things in Heaven for Earth. Movements with understanding were imperative.

For one quick moment, Abia wondered if, in some small way, this was how young Mary must have felt when she gave birth to our Lord, Jesus. The presence of God was as tangible as the light from the small oil lamp resting on the table beside Abia's bed. In His presence, she could not stand, nor did she desire to. Whether she was in a trance or asleep, she could not say. At long last, her many questions were being answered.

This heavenly awareness was to come through a series of clips from scenes of the past. The understanding and discernment given by the Holy Spirit came from beyond her own life's experiences or intellect, leaving her no room to boast. The spiritual knowledge and sensitivity came from only one place: It was revealed by God.

All that she heard was inspired by the Holy Spirit, but it was not for her alone. She merely became the scribe and reporter. In humility, Abia wrote of the great honor given her. It was written in obedience and without regard to her own inadequacies.

C H A P T E R   3 1

Dance Lessons

"I, the Spirit of God, am about to reveal to you, Abia, secrets which have been hidden from most until such a time as this." He informed her of the dance and the lessons He wanted New Testament believers to understand.

"Like all prophecy, it is spoken from God and given to people for people to obey. Miriam, David, and some others knew in part, but the revelation you are about to receive they would be envious to be given. Yet, they were the forerunners of worship in the dance. They were among the Great Cloud of Witnesses in the upper room on that celebrated and glorious day of Pentecost. They heard the sound of the dance centuries ago and prophesied this day through their own movements as they danced. It was right and appropriate for them to witness the prophetic sound of the dance when you heard it for the first time."

"There is much for you to know, for I am doing a new thing. I will speak and you will listen, Little One. Be assured I will bring all things to your remembrance, so do not fear. I will answer your questions, but in doing so, more questions will spring forth. This is a journey. You are just beginning to know Me, and through the dance, I will teach you many things. I will educate, tutor, train, and coach you about dance, but more importantly, you will not dance alone. I am your dance partner, and I am quite good," the Holy Spirit boldly declared!

Abia could not help but smile at His self-confidence. Just as she had been about to be overwhelmed, her heart was suddenly warmed by His compassionate sense of humor. He was indeed the Comforter. His confidence brought her peace.

"Did you know we danced in The Garden with Adam and Eve?" the Holy Spirit inquired rhetorically. "It is one of the many ways one can express love." His voice signified how special those times were. "Dance became something enjoyed by the holy, but regrettably, the godless enjoyed it as well."

Passion shook His voice as He remembered how satan had perverted it. "Dance is being redeemed. It has a divine purpose, and with great consideration it will be restored. As the return of Jesus gets closer, dance will have a greater purpose and will become more and more important," He prophesied.

"I, the Holy Spirit of God, came to you in the upper room that glorious day just as Jesus had promised. Jesus knew of His limitations on Earth as a man. He could only reach but a few during His lifetime. After fulfilling His divine destiny on the cross, Jesus was able to bridge the wide chasm between Heaven and Earth to restore what had been stolen in the Garden of Eden. Relationship is what the Father has always wanted with His children. Jesus, as the second Adam, accomplished what the first Adam could not do. He fulfilled the requirement of the Law and paid the ultimate penalty for sin that could only be satisfied by becoming the sacrificial Lamb.

"Sin requires a blood offering. Jesus' death on the cross met God's requirement. He died on your behalf and on behalf of all who believe in Him. He even died for those who choose not to believe in Him and who will never know the great benefits He offered them.

"When God became a man in the likeness of Jesus, He could restore the relationship He desired with His people. As a gift to His obedient Son, the Father ordained to give to Him what every creature on Earth had—a mate. A redeemed Bride was gathered from those who satan had snared away from the Father and who were now restored back to their God. Their names are written in the Lamb's Book of Life. Everyone who repents and believes in Jesus as the Son of God, who conquered death by rising again on the third day, God will make part of the Bride of Jesus, the Christ. She is the redeemed Eve as Jesus is the redeemed Adam.

"There is always a price to be paid for a bride. Father gave up His own Son for the Bride, and Jesus gave up His own life to purchase her back." With holy pride that could only come from deity, the Holy Spirit then declared, "As a betrothal gift, the Father has presented Me, the Spirit of God, to all who follow Jesus, and now I am able to abide and tabernacle in each believer until Jesus' return. I am the guarantee or the down payment to keep Jesus' Bride faithful to Him until His return. I am the seal in her heart through which the agreement is kept. For it is through Me that she has the power to become the spotless and blameless Bride Jesus is returning for.

"Until that great and magnificent day, Jesus will be preparing a mansion for His Bride. A tremendous banqueting table will be set and made ready for the day when the Father allows Jesus to bring His Bride back to Himself. 'Behold, the Bridegroom comes!' she will hear. Being made like Jesus, she will reflect His glory.

"On that special day, the Inaugural Ball will begin. Jesus will take His collective Bride by the hand and will dance with her. The Inaugural Dance will be a formal ceremony to open or mark the beginning of the Marriage Supper of the Lamb and her permanent change of position. The dance will be the first formal act of introduction and will signify to all her official position with Jesus. She is royalty, and the Father has proclaimed it so. The Bride of Christ will share His throne to rule and reign forever and ever.

"It is necessary for dance to be redeemed from its former worldliness and evil use, for there is a divine purpose and plan. By its design, this dance includes two partners, but only one can lead. Dancing with Jesus, like becoming a Christian, requires a leader to follow. It allows His dance partner opportunities to practice following Him. As the partner of Christ and joint heir to the throne, the Bride's responsibilities will include being a ruler, governing, and decreeing the will and purposes of God. Dancing on Earth provides an opportunity to do on Earth as it is in Heaven.

"This, Abia, is the mission of the prophetic sound of the dance you heard that glorious day in the upper room. As a prophetic dancer, the Bride of Christ will be telling others, 'Jesus is alive and the Spirit of God is alive in me!'" He divulged excitedly.

Abia could hardly comprehend what was being spoken by the Holy Spirit for the magnitude of it was too grand to grasp. What manner of love the Father had bestowed on her! To be part of the Body of Christ, to be considered the Bride of Christ, and to house the Holy Spirit of God Himself was more than mere flesh and blood could realize.

Abia's spirit instinctively craved the ability to respond to the incredible revelation by lowering herself before such a high and lofty God. Love and honor have been offered to humankind in an unprecedented way: men, women, and children must simply believe Jesus to be the true Son of God. To believe in Him is an honor, but to dance with Him—unimaginable!

The Holy Spirit seemed delighted with the reverence Abia showed Him as He continued His teachings. "'And it will come about after this that I will pour out My Spirit on all mankind; and your sons and daughters will prophesy, your old men will dream dreams, your young men will see visions. Even on the male and female servants I will pour out My Spirit in those days.'" The Holy Spirit recited Joel the prophet of old, as well as Jesus when He spoke to His disciples: "'But an hour is coming, and now is, when the true worshipers will worship the Father in spirit and truth; for such people the Father seeks to be His worshipers. God is spirit, and those who worship Him must worship in spirit and truth.'

"Redeemed, divinely inspired dance speaks the truth of the promises of the Father, the completed work of the cross, and the assurance of the Holy Spirit, with Jesus' words fulfilled and proclaimed by each dance.

"The prophetic sound of the dance heard by the Bride of Christ means a change in her identity. She is neither Jew nor Greek, there is neither slave nor free person, there is neither male nor female; for you are all one in Christ Jesus. And if you belong to Christ, then you are Abraham's descendants, heirs according to promise. You are a chosen race, a royal priesthood, a holy nation, a people for God's own possession, so that you may proclaim the Excellencies of Him who has called you out of darkness into His marvelous light.

"The Bride must not only behave as royalty, but she must know she is royalty. As royalty, she has Jesus' authority, which includes the right and power to enforce rules and give orders. Being granted His authority involves having the power to act on Jesus' behalf with official permission to do so. The Bride will be an official body that is set up by the King of all kings to administer in areas of activity in Heaven and on Earth. She has the ability to gain the respect of others and influence or control what they do. With legitimate power, she will establish precedent or principles.

With godly wisdom, knowledge, skill, and experience, she is worthy of respect and can hold her head high without shame when her identity is fully recognized.

"Divine protocol will be followed. Each movement will have appropriate procedures, rules, and practices, including a code of behaviors that are correct, pure, and appropriate. They will only be accomplished with My assistance.

"Until the Inauguration Day when the Bride will dance with her King face to face, she will learn and practice this on Earth," the Holy Spirit proceeded. "The Bride must learn to walk the fine line between being friends of God and never forgetting He is I AM. He is royalty and holy, yet approachable and kind.

"There are certain conventions or rules of correct behavior that must be learned for ceremonial occasions. I, the Holy Spirit, will partner with the Bride and will lead her in this new dance. I will instruct, guide, and direct her in proper dance etiquette and behavior, which will bring respect from others and will draw all attention to Jesus.

"I am the Holy Spirit, but the Bride will know me by other names as well. I am the Helper; the Spirit of Jesus; the Spirit of Life; the Spirit of Truth; the Spirit of Holiness; the Spirit of Judgment; the Spirit of Fire; the Oil of Joy; the Spirit of Grace; the Spirit of Glory; the Guide; the Great Counselor; the Spirit of Wisdom, Understanding, Counsel, Power, Knowledge; and the Spirit of the Fear of the Lord. I am also her Teacher, and as Esther before her, she will be more than ready when she is presented to Jesus on that magnificent day. I am not a poor substitute for Jesus. In fact, I am the Holy Spirit who is the third person of the Trinity and the spiritual force of God. Remember, I am also a wonderful dancer, and I cannot fail. I will teach her to dance an eternal dance with her Beloved, Jesus," the Instructor persisted.

"Jesus loves weddings and the closeness they promise," The Holy Spirit disclosed. "His first earthly miracle was at a wedding. It showed to all how I, Holy Spirit, am the New Wine offered to those who will drink. The focus of Jesus' death dance allowed a betrothal of marriage between Him and His Bride. He has made sure all has been done. He is focused and intent on having His Bride, the one His Father promised. The joy of being wed to her made it possible for Him to endure the cross. Jesus' crucifixion dance was an extremely intimate act. It was an extremely passionate proof of His love for His Bride and obedience of the Father. His obedience at the cross allowed Me, the Holy Spirit, to be brought individually to her for the first time. I am the Wine that seals the deal. It is all quite romantic!

"Abia, try to picture how Heaven bent low to kiss Earth. Mercy reached out to touch grace. The created could abide in the Creator and the Creator in the created. Jesus, the Lover, found a lover to love. Love danced to Calvary so Love could one day dance with His Bride at the Wedding Feast.

"There will be a great and glorious day when the Bride will dance with her Groom. In her eyes will be a total reflection of Jesus. At the end of their dance, when the perfect moment in time occurs when all is completed and redemption is completely fulfilled, Jesus will face the Father in the Holy City. With a regal bow, Jesus will proclaim to the Father the fulfillment of His earthly prayer:

'I have manifested Your name to the men whom You gave Me out of the world; they were Yours and You gave them to Me, and they have kept Your word. Now they have come to know that everything You have given Me is from You; for the words which You gave Me I have given to them; and they received them and truly understood that I came forth from You, and they believed that You sent Me. I ask on their behalf; I do no ask on behalf of the world, but of those whom You have given Me; for they are

Yours; and all things that are Mine are Yours, and Yours are Mine; and I have been glorified in them. I am no longer in the world; and yet they themselves are in the world, and I come to You. Holy Father, keep them in Your name, the name which You have given Me, that they may be one even as We are. While I was with them, I was keeping them in Your name which You have given Me; and I guarded them and not one of them perished but the son of perdition, so that the Scripture would be fulfilled.

But now I come to You; and these things I speak in the world so that they may have My joy made full in themselves. I have given them Your word; and the world has hated them, because they are not of the world, even as I am not of the world. I do not ask You to take them out of the world, but to keep them from the evil one. They are not of the world, even as I am not of the world. Sanctify them in the truth; Your word is truth. As You sent Me into the world, I also have sent them into the world. For their sakes I sanctify Myself, that they themselves also may be sanctified in truth.

I do not ask on behalf of these alone, but for those also who believe in Me through their word; that they may all be one; even as You, Father, are in Me and I in You, that they also may be in Us, so that the world may believe that You sent Me.

The glory which You have given Me I have given to them, that they may be one, just as We are one; I in them and You in Me, that they may be perfected in unity, so that the world may know that You sent Me, and loved them, even as You have loved Me. Father, I desire that they also, whom You have given Me, be with Me where I am, so that they may see My glory which You have given Me, for You loved Me before the foundation of the world.

O righteous Father, although the world has not known You, yet I have known You; and these have known that You sent Me; and I have made Your name known to them, and will make it known, so that the love with which You loved Me may be in them, and I in them.'

"Taking His beloved Bride by the hand, Jesus will move her toward a beautiful bridge with the river of life running beneath. The bridge will be flanked by cherubim and flaming swords flashing back and forth, guarding its entrance. As Jesus and His Bride approach, the cherubim will stand at ease for the first time in history from guarding the tree of life.

"On the bridge peak, Jesus and His Bride will wait. Jesus will say to His Father, 'I present back to You, with a heart full of love and devotion, Your Son and the Bride You have chosen for Me. Together, we redeem everything lost to You, Father. Today we come back home to You.' Jesus and His Bride will joyously run hand in hand over the bridge, returning to the Garden of Eden and into the opened arms of the Father."

There was a long silence after Holy Spirit spoke of the day when Jesus and His Bride would be presented back to the Father. Abia's silence came as a result of trying to comprehend the wonderful day; the Holy Spirit's silence came as the yearning and longing for the day overwhelmed Him.

CHAPTER 32

Counterfeit to the Original

The Holy Spirit spoke to Abia at times as though they were best friends having conversation over hot tea. Other times, she heard no sound at all, but her spirit was inspired with words of knowledge and the wisdom to understand them as He disclosed more and more about the dance.

Deeper revelation of the dance came as He taught her to listen with her spirit. He said that spiritual things must be spiritually discerned. The flesh could not understand the ways of God. If dance was to be understood, the worshipers' spirits would have to be awakened by the Holy Spirit Himself. They would need to follow Him by studying His steps and movements, but also His purpose and intention.

The Holy Spirit wanted Abia to study the counterfeit, the dark, and the perverse use of dance to discover the opposite and true intention of dance. "For a true counterfeit illegally imitates the original." The lessons were not for Abia alone. He was speaking to her personally, but also to her collectively, as the Bride of Christ. She was humbled to be spoken of and referred to as the Beloved of Jesus.

When Abia began to study the dance that had brought about the death of the last of the prophets from the old Covenant, John the Baptist, it stood out as rather strange in light of the other types of dances and dancers she knew.

From Abia's earliest memory, she had heard stories of Miriam, with a timbrel in her hand, and how she danced with great celebration and jubilation after the Jewish people crossed over the Red Sea. She witnessed the incredible miracles of deliverance by the hand of God, and she danced in remembrance of that extraordinary event. She was the first to dance to what was happening around her.

There were also amazing stories of King David. He was a king who had danced with all his might before the Lord when he brought the Ark of the Covenant into the city of David. The tangible presence of God Almighty had found a home with His people after 200 years of separation. By example, King David used dance to set into place the order of worship for God's people to follow.

With that in mind, Abia's question remained, *Why would the Lord allow me to see the beheading of John the Baptist?* She wondered, *If this unsanctified dancer, Salome, and her unholy dance presented a fraudulent or negative impression of what dance was created to be, what can the Originator of the dance be saying to me?*

The Holy Spirit led her to study the life and ways of the people involved in the dances Abia had witnessed. By examining them, greater revelation came as to what dance was intended to be. To be able to dance at the Inaugural Banquet Feast, dance indeed had to be understood, redeemed, and purified.

The death of John involved more than the use of seduction to gain what was desired. This dance was complex: life, kings, kingdoms, and authority were all at stake. The Holy Spirit showed Abia how the intention of the heart and character of a person can inspire good or evil and equally impact them both. Dance is powerful. It was not an insignificant part of this tragic story. In the hands of the wicked it was used as a weapon to murder.

There should be one standard by which to measure everything, and His name is Jesus, the Holy Spirit reminded her. Dancers, kings, and all others should use Jesus as the benchmark after which to pattern themselves. Discernment became much easier when He was the gauge. Having a greater understanding of Jesus was the means by which critical assessments of people and circumstances could be made. With Jesus as the mirror, the true meaning of the dances Abia had witnessed could be understood.

Herod offered up to half his kingdom to a dancer because Herod's physical pleasures were of greater importance to him than his kingdom, making him an earthy and foolish ruler. He had accepted the prostitution of his stepdaughter for his own fleshly and perverted gratification. The dance became a performance. It became a means to entertain and be entertained, to seduce and be seduced, and it was used for wickedness, not holiness. The dance was allowed to become a weapon used in the wrong hands, bringing destruction.

The Holy Spirit told Abia, "Herod Antipas was in direct opposition to what a true and godly king should be. He was a counterfeit king. Jesus, on the other hand, is the true King of all Heaven and Earth. He has legitimate authority over both. Those who have been born anew through the resurrection power of Jesus and the completed work of the cross are spiritually adopted into the family of God. They are legitimate heirs to His throne by the death dance of Jesus Christ. As joint heirs to His Kingdom, the same authority given to Him is given to them.

"When worshipers dance, they are interceding and are warring on behalf of God's Kingdom with authorized, legitimate authority. There are no limits when people intercede for the will of the Father, the Son, and Me, the Holy Spirit. We will move Heaven and Earth when there is agreement with Us.

"The new prophetic dance is used to bring increase to the Kingdom of God. Jesus died for the people of God, and it is His desire that none will perish, but that all will have eternal life. To dance out of your loving relationship with Him requires that He lead and move you in the direction of His heart. Be passionate about those things He is passionate about, namely His Bride and doing the will of the Father.

"When I, the Holy Spirit, instruct dancers to dance, they will have His heart and should keep His will ever before them. They will be Kingdom-minded, and with salvation for the people as the ultimate mission and goal, pleasing the true King is assured.

"Herod allowed dance in his palace; My dwelling place is in the believers, who have become temples in which I can abide. They are allowed and encouraged to dance in Jesus' presence because it is for the edification and salvation of others. It will bring about destruction of the enemy and cause the demons to flee. The dancer's reward is manifested in a variety of ways, including healing, prosperity, wholeness, deliverance, peace, and freedom, among the many treasures God has promised. Dancing can reach into the heavens and pull down all those things the Father has provided for humankind when it is done in faith and by My power."

The Holy Spirit unraveled yet more mysteries to Abia, "While caution should be used, not to perform or to make a show of dance, dance as worship can bring personal and corporate gain. It will bring forth life and life more abundantly.

"Reflecting on Herodias, wife of Herod Antipas and mother of Salome, we can see that she had a profound hatred of the prophet of God, and her refusal to repent for her sins opened wide the gate of her spirit. This allowed easy access to a multitude of evil spirits, including a haughty spirit, a lying and perverse spirit, and a spirit of harlotry. She was not under the covering of God's covenant and protection.

"With manipulation and control as her weapons, Herodias used others around her in a dramatic guise of celebrating her husband's birth, all the while planning John's death. She knew the power and value of dance, but she used it for evil. She dishonored God's anointed intention for dance. In doing so, she brought dishonor to her husband, her own daughter, and herself. As a pawn in the hands of satan, she killed the prophet and attempted to silence his prophetic voice.

Herodias' daughter, Salome, used dance for her own reward as well. She prostituted herself and the art of dancing by using them for dishonorable, criminal, and immoral profit and gains. Salome was a counterfeit dancer. Her dance was anointed by evil, and it produced evil fruit. She was self-focused, not God focused. Her movements were driven and directed by vanity and pride with self-promotion in mind. She used something God created, perverted it, and made a weapon of death from it.

"I know the value and power of a believer's dance for I lead it, and I use it for good for the Kingdom of God. Those I will call to minister to God in the dance, I will anoint and empower to dance with My power. These chosen ones will hear the sound of the dance, just as you did, Abia. They will take their places among dancers who have an anointing to intercede on behalf of others and ask for life instead of death. This dance troop will be a mighty force, spirited and equipped by Jesus Himself and empowered by the power of God.

"The blood of Jesus has redeemed the dance; it is made righteous, godly, and holy. While Herodias used her daughter for her own selfish gain, the heavenly Father will allow His daughters and sons to dance a dance that ministers life, healing, redemption, revelation, and increase to His Church. Love will be their motivation, just as it was with Jesus when He danced the death dance all the way to the cross.

"Herodias knew dance would bring about a reward because it was used as entertainment. Jesus invokes a reward when dancers are obedient to the dance for Him. He will reward them with intimacy and with a greater love for Him and for others than they could ever imagine. They will hear His voice and together will move in this dance and do incredible things. He chose to allow their dance to be an offering of sacrifice that is holy and acceptable in His sight. He is pleased by worship and pours back into them His compassion for His people. They become His partner, and as a result, will bring forth a greater harvest of souls to His Church.

"Until that glorious day when the Bride takes her place at Jesus' side, the Bride has much to learn. God will use the dance to give life to the prophetic and speak prophetically to the people. The counterfeit dance killed the prophet, but God is making His holy dancer a demonstrative prophet. Dancers will indeed be an inspired mouthpiece of the will of God through movement. This weapon in the hands of God is more powerful than the Bride knows.

"The believers who dance in warfare and intercession will bring about death to the enemy and his schemes because the dancers have gained an audience with the King of kings. Dance is indeed a weapon, for it is designed for inflicting harm on the enemy of God and his schemes. Each dance step is an unexpected means to gain an advantage over the enemy and for defending themselves and others in the Kingdom. Through obedience and submission, the dance will bring God glory. After all, it is by invitation and with His complete permission. While it may be beautiful and graceful at times, it is deadly and devastating to the demonic. Godly dance movements persuade, influence, and promote the desires of a loving and caring God for everyone's benefit.

"When the dancers rush to the throne room of God with personal or corporate petitions, they will be granted," the Holy Spirit said. "Jesus' death and the New Covenant made by the shedding of His blood make it so. Those petitions are made with delegated authority and power. When believers dance as King David, with clean hands and a pure heart, there is alignment with God. Agreement with His Word brings unity. In unity, God will command a blessing. The dancers will be successful at turning the face of God toward them because He cannot resist the sweet, fragrant smell of worship. The curses will be turned to blessings. The blind will see. The lame will walk. The impossible will be made possible. It is just as true for dancers as anyone else: they have not for they ask not. Ask, seek, and knock, and the heavenly doors will be opened.

"God is in the business of restoring, redeeming, and sanctifying all things. The morally corrupted dance will be rescued from the hands of the enemy and made pure through the purification of Jesus' own blood. It will be liberated and delivered to its original design. The restoration is simply taking what is God's in the first place, using it for His glory, and giving it back to Him. Dance, which was once considered something to do to celebrate the goodness of God, is much more.

'Praise the Lord! Sing to the Lord a new song, and His praise in the congregation of the godly ones. Let Israel be glad in his Maker; let the sons of Zion rejoice in their King. Let them praise His name with dancing; let them sing praises to Him with timbrel and lyre. For the Lord takes pleasure in His people; He will beautify the afflicted ones with salvation. Let the godly ones exult in glory; let them sing for joy on their beds. Let the high praises of God be in their mouth, and a two-edged sword in their hand, to execute vengeance on the nations and punishment on the peoples, to bind their kings with chains and their nobles with fetters of iron, to execute on them the judgment written; this is an honor for all His godly ones. Praise the Lord!'

"David knew the power of dance as a weapon. He once said, *'Blessed be the Lord, my rock, who trains my hands for war, and my fingers for battle.'* The Spirit of God, will guide and direct the movements of the dancers' hands and fingers while dancing. The Word of the Lord is a weapon, and so are the dancers' dances. Combined they become a powerful tool against the enemy and a wonderful key to entering into the chambers of Jesus' own heart. Dance with Him. He is the Lord of the Dance. David learned this and so must dancers of the New Covenant," The Holy Spirit urged.

Abia had been entrusted with the knowledge of the power and weaponry that dance is. She was chosen when she was only four years old, and her destiny was set in place through a series of dreams that foretold the future. Abia had been privileged to be allowed to see into the spiritual realm and witness the immediate results that dance intercession can bring. The Lord opened the door by showing Abia the power of dance when Samuel was protected from harm's way. Her heart motive, when she danced and interceded for Samuel, was based primarily on her love for him and her trust in God's ability to protect. It was what propelled her to dance on his behalf.

That is the sound of the new dance. It is one saturated in the same love and compassion that moved Jesus to His death dance. It is the new dance sound that Jesus had heard and one that Abia also heard—partnering with Him in the dance to the sound of Heaven in order to change Earth.

Abia had witnessed the obscene dance of Salome and Jesus' own death dance at the cross. He had trusted her with both just as He trusts anyone He calls.

The Holy Spirit continued His instruction. "Dancers must always remember Jesus' death dance most of all. They are to remember all of His moves and actions and His purpose and destiny when He danced. This new breed of dancer is to be purposeful and intentional just like Jesus. He spilled His own blood for those who believe in Him so that they could have the privilege of partnering with Him in this life's dance. It was one of redemption and of grace. It was history-altering and timely. This new thing He trusts worshipers with, this new dance, is not to be regarded as anything less than holy."

Abia had been chosen because she possessed the heart of a worshiper, and the Holy Spirit knew that, in time, she would mature into a woman in love with her Beloved. Jesus' words were precious to her, and her character reflected His. The Spirit then spoke to her a personalized version of Isaiah 61, which Jesus had quoted as His life purpose. It had become the life purpose of Abia and all those who dance with Jesus:

> *The Spirit of the Lord God is upon you, Dancers of the Most High, because the Lord has anointed you to bring good news to the afflicted; He has sent you to bind up the brokenhearted, to proclaim liberty to captives and freedom to prisoners; to proclaim the favorable year of the Lord and the day of vengeance of our God; to comfort all who mourn, to grant those who mourn in Zion, giving them a garland instead of ashes, the oil of gladness instead of mourning, the mantle of praise instead of a spirit of fainting. So they will be called oaks of righteousness, the planting of the lord, that He may be glorified.*

"This is the calling of all worshipers and of worshipers who dance," explained the Holy Spirit. They are members of the remnant of those long ago who heard the sound and danced, but there are others."

Abia was to do with dance what Adam had been instructed to do in The Garden: be fruitful and multiply dance to others. She would instruct those whom Jesus would call. Jesus would be her only husband, for it was in Abia's own heart to remain single for Him and His calling, but she would become a mother. Abia would become a mother of the faith and one who taught dance by its original design and intention to others.

CHAPTER 33

Prophetic Sound and Movement

Deeper revelation for dance came from the Lord regularly. Abia became the student, with the Holy Spirit as her teacher. Fresh revelation came to her on an ongoing basis. For her to be able to instruct others, He had to teach her. Her life was devoted to Him, and He was completely devoted to her. The prophet Hosea had proclaimed centuries ago a truth that Abia adopted as her own. "'It will come about in that day,' declares the Lord, *'That you will call Me Ishi* [My Husband].'" Her life was wonderfully full, and in true Jewish fashion, the husband taught his wife about the ways of God. Abia's Ishi taught her.

He explained how from the beginning, movement and sound worked together. The Spirit of God was moving over the formless void and darkness that was over the surface of the deep. As God spoke, the heavens and the Earth were created. God is the Creator who creates things and makes things happen. When the

Spirit of God moved, hovered, and fluttered by the wind, breath, and mind of God, darkness moved out of His way.

The Holy Spirit explained, "When a Spirit-filled dancer moves by the Word of God, darkness, all shadows, and all secret places of the enemy have to flee. All empty places must move to make room for an infilling of what God considers good. Confusion, chaos, wastelands, and places of vanity must give way to God's better way. He separated, severed, and made a distinction between darkness and light. Believers must do the same.

"Since humankind was created by sound and by the movement of God the Father, Jesus the Son, and Me, the Holy Spirit, humankind has the same sounds within them. This accumulative sound is mighty to the tearing down of all strongholds of the enemy. The harmonious blending of sound and movement commands personal, corporate, governmental, national, and worldwide blessings. The prophetic sound of dance movements creates just as God created in Genesis. Prophetic utterances and commands of instruction or warnings are given with each dance activity. Warlike energy to accomplish and administer in power are executed by sound waves coming from dance movements. The manifestation of the glory of God, with all its abundance, splendor, riches, creativity, miracles, healing, provision, salvations, and deliverances, is accessible to those who wait upon the Spirit of God.

"Jesus will speak through dance movements. Each will be a language of movement just as living as the spoken Word of God. This language of movement and gestures is a sound of Heaven converging upon the Earth. When that sound is awakened by the Holy Spirit, movements in the dance, coupled with a broken and contrite heart, will attract the presence of God. His head will be turned in that direction when dance is in unison with Him.

"All those who are My dancers will be messengers who go after God's heart and speak through their movements what is on the mind or heart of God. Dancers give expression to that which is received in the spiritual realm.

"The movements of the dance disrupt and disturb the prince of the power of the air. Satan's airspace is invaded by the prophetic dance sound waves that are made when dance movements occur. This sound brings disorder and chaos to the enemy's camp. When the sounds of Heaven marry the sounds of the prophetic on Earth, the collective sound deafens the enemy. All predators scramble from every victim at the roar of the Lion of Judah. Darkness trembles and runs from God's glorious and awful majesty as the sound of lightning flashes in all directions.

"Every disease and sickness which is called by a name must bow before the sound of the name which is above every other name" declared the Holy Spirit, rejoicing. "The sound of My powerful rushing Wind whirls the enemy from his place. This prophetic sound of the dance brings about change in the spirit realm, which brings about changes in the world. Worshipers will dance into battle, but the battle belongs to Me. Authority to speak forth the truths of God will be given. Prayers of intercession will make divine historic changes and will make predictions of the future.

Because dancers called of God dance with Me in faith, complete trust and confidence are a must. Dancers cannot trust in movements, but in Me, the One who created all things and through whom nothing is impossible. Having faith in their own faith will not be sufficient. Faith must be based solely on Me. I will speak and their faith response will be the Spirit's language of dance. In doing so, life will prophetically be spoken into every circumstance."

Abia was determined to be a good student of what the Lord had revealed to her. She danced whenever she had the opportunity, but now danced with purpose, faith, and growing understanding.

Dance, by its name, implies action. With new understanding, Abia took action to dance with Her Beloved. With each action, faith and knowledge of the power of the dance became real to her as never before.

When Abia heard that Judith and Abraham were expecting a baby, Abia danced with joy all around her sister and proclaimed the Word of God over the child while still in the womb. Remembering the need to know God's Word and make agreement with it, she laid her hands on her sister's stomach. Abia pronounced to the unborn child: "For You formed the little one's inward parts; You are weaving this one in her mother's womb for she or he is fearfully and wonderfully made!" Months later, Samuel John Ben-David was born healthy, and his first action was to lift his hands in the air, as if he were a worshiper already!

While visiting Judith and the baby one day, Abia became very concerned about Judith's mother-in-law, Mora. Abia had a word of knowledge about Mora and the inner struggle she faced daily since early childhood. Mora's gossiping habit was a result of trying to be noticed and accepted by others. Mora had experienced much rejection as an unwanted adopted child who had been passed from one relative to the next. She suffered greatly from unworthiness and did not understand how precious she was to God.

When Abia returned home late that afternoon, she was burdened for Mora. Abia danced and prayed prayers of intercession for her. One of the movements she felt inclined to do was to form her hands, with joined palms and fingers outstretched, into the shape of a crown. As she swirled around and around in a circle, she finally knelt down on one knee, and as if Mora were in front of her, Abia placed the crown upon her head. Abia felt as if the Holy Spirit wanted her prayer for Mora to embrace a new way of thinking as portrayed by the crown being placed on her head. In the days ahead, Abia got word from Judith that Mora had received Jesus as her Savior and that she already saw the changes in her thinking as her hardened heart softened with the knowledge of Jesus' love.

Abia was also praying and dancing on behalf of Akil, the social planner, who rejected any mention of Jesus or any type of religion, believing he had no need for it. As often as possible, Abia would make inquiries about Akil in the marketplace when the slaves and servants came to buy for the palace kitchen. No good news was reported about Akil. She continued to lift him up in prayer, but Akil's own will was in the way of his receiving all that God wanted for him. The Word of God says, "You have not because you ask not," and she was determined to ask and ask again if necessary.

In the winter, Abia's mother, Hannah's fever peaked so high that everyone thought she would die as a result. Two days had passed, and Abia finally convinced her father to leave his wife long enough to get some much-needed rest for himself. With the room empty, but for the two of them, Abia began her dance of intercession on behalf of her sick mother. Abia declared God's own words over her mother: "She will not die, but live, and tell of the works of the Lord."

Suddenly, with her feet planted firmly on the floor, Abia started to move her hand as the cruel soldiers had done with Jesus as they took a whip to His back. "Jesus bore stripes on His back and shed His blood for healing, so in the name of Jesus, Momma, be healed because it is the will of the Father. By the power of Holy Spirit and by the name of Jesus, be healed!" Abia commanded. Hannah's fever broke the next day!

Abia also learned something incredible. She learned that dancing with Jesus brought to her peace as she had never known it. When she danced with Jesus, she felt whole, and dancing was a wonderful gate into His presence. In Him there was help to handle life and its struggles. As time marched on, Abia could say as the Shulammite woman of long ago, who declared of her bridegroom, "He is my beloved and this is my friend."

CHAPTER 34

Dance Onward, Warrior Bride

Daylight burst over the horizon each morning, and the months passed. Abia's mind could hardly absorb all that was revealed to her. From her window, the world seemed the same. The marketplace was busy with early morning shoppers. Dogs barked at the unknown, and the smell of dyes boiling in the kitchen room permeated the air. Roman soldiers patrolled the streets, and people gave them a wide path when they passed. Laughter could be heard, but if one listened more closely, so could cries.

Life continued as ususal, but Abia would never be the same. One could not experience the reality of God and remain the same. At long last the questions that plagued her about Salome's dance and Jesus' death dance were finally answered. Peace flooded her soul. An inner excitement for the purpose and destiny God had for her and her prophetic dance burned within her.

With each month that came and went, life was challenging and would have been impossible to endure without God's grace and help. The desperation she sometimes felt was much like her dream, when she was only four and the man of her dreams had let go of her hand, leaving her with a sense of helplessness and despair.

Fortunately, that dream was one that did not come true! In reality, she discovered that He never leaves, forsakes, or loosens His grip on those He loves. With the world full of trouble and trials in every direction, holding His hand was the only safe thing to do. By putting her trust in Him, He became the lifter of her head. Trouble still came, but the outlook of being firmly planted in the palm of His hand gave new perspective and hope for the future. That reality would bring much comfort in the years ahead.

The disciples were spread far and wide, preaching and teaching the Good News of Jesus. They suffered horribly for believing in Jesus. Yet, it seemed the more the Church was persecuted, the more it grew, much to the astonishment of the government and religious leaders.

Over and over again, the Lord allowed Abia to dance in intercession on behalf of Jesus' disciples and for believers everywhere. Abia danced publicly and privately with the leading of Holy Spirit for personal and corporate needs. She danced on behalf of her town and government as to bring about the changes that would lead to integrity and moral purity. Her intercession included prayers for national and worldwide revelation of Jesus and His teachings for all to come to a saving knowledge of Jesus. She prayed all through the movements of the dance.

Abia declared with her body, mind, and spirit the words of God each time she danced. The Holy Spirit was maturing her in the new sound of the dance. She became more sensitive to His voice as He prophetically spoke through her and the dances He gave to her. He instructed her to dance the faith dance and not be moved when her eyes did not often see evidence of much change around her. He assured her that faith in Him was all He was looking for; He would handle the rest.

Jesus had spoken to His disciples, and Abia applied His teaching to herself—"He who has ears to hear let him hear." The new prophetic sound of the dance made her develop a keen sense of hearing. She found that when she leaned close to her Beloved she could hear the new sounds and dance accordingly. The new sounds were the clues to how she should dance. When Abia heard and added her agreement, He commanded a blessing to each one. As she matured in her faith by dancing her life's dance with Him, her hearing increased, and the sound she danced to and from became clearer as her faith grew.

Abia began to hear the prophetic sounds of the rod of Christ's rule and authority coming into the earthly realm while she awaited His return. She declared His power and ability with each move of her dance. She was moved by the sounds of the cadence from the war horses when a battle ensued. She heard the sounds of the enemies as they approached, and she danced God's protection. She could prophetically hear the sounds of the ancient barriers being destroyed and ancient walls crumbling. Abia heard the sounds of weapons being forged against the Church, but not prospering. She heard the sounds God makes at night when He goes without sleep.

Answers to prayers could be heard as golden bowls were filled. She began to hear the sound of the chambers of His heart opening for her and the Church as their love for Him grew. The heavenly storehouse creaked open as Abia prayed for His provision to meet the needs of His people. Ancient pathways and gates were being unlocked as she danced in intercession for greater intimacy for Jesus and His Bride.

Victory could be heard in God's camp when more lost souls turned their hearts to God. Sounds of the wounded and brokenhearted could be heard. Sounds of spiritual fire, wind, and rain could be heard, just as in the days when a pillar of smoke and fire had led God's people through the wilderness.

The Father's laugh could be heard when His enemies approached. The many names of God could be heard to give her intercession greater impact and power when she came into agreement to each one.

Sometimes Abia could hear the groaning sounds of Jesus' intercession on humankind's behalf, especially when the people resisted the help of God. Hearing Jesus's heart sing for joy when they let Him into theirs was a glorious sound. God inhabited the praises of His people, and she discovered that the sound of generational strongholds being broken and dry bones coming together was an astounding sound

Shifting and transformation had a sound. The Lion of Judah's roar shook her to her knees. As Abia raised her arms, as David had, she could hear the thud from stones hitting the "Goliaths" that were coming against God's people.

With prophetic ears and by the power of the Holy Spirit, Abia was allowed to hear the cries of the poor, the hungry, the hurting, and the helpless. Justice had a sound that shattered the lies of injustice from the enemy. God gave her ears to hear false prophets and false witnesses. She was given the honor of being able to hear the sound of God's hands breaking the arms of humankind's enemy. At the touch of those same strong hands, she heard the cries of the hopeless quieted.

The ability to hear Scriptures increased. Abia began to hear the sound of His footsteps on the stormiest seas of her life, and she could hear the sound of demons fleeing at His command. Abia was allowed to hear His whisper calling her to go into the Outer Court, the Inner Court, and the Holy of Holies. When she battled on behalf of others, she heard the sound of captives being released from their prisons. He allowed her, by the power of the

Holy Spirit, to hear the swords of angels being unleashed to do battle in the heavenly realm for God's promises to be manifested on Earth.

Spiritual ears were quickened for His revelation and His Word. God's breath had a sound when it entered someone who had once been strangled by an invisible enemy that desired to keep His people bound in religion and not relationship. Abia was often given the privilege of hearing in the Spirit the sound of a drop of blood as it rolled from the stripes on Jesus' back when she was praying for someone's emotional and physical healing.

Hearing the sound from God was vital to faith. The apostle Paul taught the Roman Christians, *"Faith comes from hearing, and hearing by the word of Christ."*

Following the Holy Spirit as she danced was one of the most exciting things Abia had ever experienced. It was amazing to her that God's hands, which held the Earth and galaxies, were extended to humankind as they joined with Him in the dance. She prayed that she would never take for granted this privilege.

Abia discovered that an amazing benefit came when she danced. God brought about much healing in her heart each time she danced before Him. The good work that was started when she became a believer and was baptized continued. As her relationship with God the Father, God the Son, and God the Holy Spirit became richer, she gained more and more freedom and liberty.

Poor Salome had danced with her many veils, which left her totally uncovered and resulted in the death of a prophet. But death could not hold down the King of kings. He was alive and so were those who believed in Him. On the day Jesus was crucified, the veil was rent so believers in Jesus could dance before Him and with Him.

Unfortunately, some refused to believe and had found no covering from God. So it was with Salome, whom Abia had heard had recently died. Salome, who had been successful at turning the heart of Herod by using dance as a murder weapon, had now suffered an ironic death. It was reported that, as Salome was walking over the somewhat shallow part of a frozen lake, the ice broke suddenly before her feet. She fell into the water up to her neck. As the frozen ice fragments danced back and forth, Salome's head was severed, leaving her head on a platter of ice.

Regarding Herod Antipas, Herodias finally convinced him to go to Rome and demand of Emperor Caligula that he be granted the title of king. But Herodias' brother, Herod Agrippa, who was a companion of the Emperor Caligula, tricked his sister out of the crown she so passionately pursued. Emperor Caligula gave Herod Antipas' land away to Agrippa, had him removed from his office and position of power, and had him banished to Lugdunum (Lyon) in Gaul.

Many times in the days, months, and years that followed, the believers' only refuge was found in the comforting arms of Christ. It was true of Abia's parents, who were allowed the honor of holding on their laps three grandsons apiece from Samuel and Mary as well as from Judith and Abraham. The provision of so many grandsons helped soften the blow of Abia's decision not to marry and, therefore, not to produce for them more grandchildren. Nonetheless, it did not stop their prayers for Abia to change her mind one day and make room in her heart for some nice Jewish man. Yet her parents grew to understand her calling and valued what she was doing and how she was furthering God's Kingdom in a very special way.

Turbulent times faced the Ben-David family in the days ahead. They rested in the knowledge that, because of the hope they had in Jesus, nothing would separate them from His love or their loved ones in this life or the next.

More than once, dance seemed like the last thing Abia wanted to do as the unrest all around them seemed to take control. But when she turned from the world and turned toward Jesus, she found rest from life's struggles and pain. Abia always found peace in her Ishi's arms, especially when they danced. It was then that she would hear the new heavenly dance sound once more and dance with the Lord of the Dance. As they danced, He confirmed to her His love, giving her hope and direction in life. She was His dancer, and her desire to minister in the dance pleased Him.

Life made so much more sense to her as a Christian. The knowledge of being loved by her Creator was incredible. He promised that life's problems would not go away, but He also promised that He would hold her hand as they walked and danced through this life on Earth together. Her hope and purpose in life came from Him because all the world could offer her was a counterfeit or a poor substitute to what He offered.

During one of the times, as she danced before Him, she saw in her spirit others who were partnering with her in the dance. She saw millions of them of all ages and both sexes, of all shapes and all nationalities, swirling around and around with Jesus as their lead. It was hard for her to imagine millions of believers who would hear the sound of the dance and respond.

Just then, she heard a knock on at her door. As she peered through the window, she saw three young women and two young men. Abia had seen them many times before in the marketplace and at feasts and special festivals. They had hearts for worship and a tremendous love for Jesus. As she opened the door, the small group stood before her. They said, "God sent us to enquire from the one who hears the prophetic sound of the dance and dances with Jesus."

Abia knew it had begun.

THE END

About Linda Fitzpatrick

Linda Fitzpatrick is wife, mother, Mimi (of two precious grandchildren), and a woman who loves Jesus and has heard His call to dance and to minister in the dance for the past nineteen years. Her journey to dance began when several women from Fellowship of Living Praise Church desired to worship Jesus in a more intimate way. It was soon discovered that many of the women longed to have a greater, more intimate relationship with Jesus, but life experiences made intimacy with anyone challenging. A weekly Bible study was formed to study their dance partner, Jesus, resulting in a dance team finally being formed seven years later. She has personally experienced the restoration power of dance when it is married with the Word of God as the Holy Spirit ushers healing down the aisle to the wounded soul. For the last twelve years, Fellowship of Living Praise Dance Ministry Team has learned to dance following the Holy Spirit, minister in the dance by Jesus, with the Father's fullest blessings. From the foothills of northern Georgia and other states, to Ottawa, Canada, and Ghana, Africa, Linda has shared Jesus' love and the importance of prophetic intercession dance as a weapon used for the Kingdom of God. As Prayer Minister Coordinator and team leader at her church, Linda's heart is to see the wounded healed, the broken restored, and the Bride of Christ victoriously dancing.

lindafitzpatrick2011@gmail.com
www.worshiperswindow.com
Twitter: soundofthedance
Facebook: Linda Fitzpatrick and Dancing With Jesus

DESTINY IMAGE PUBLISHERS, INC.

"Promoting Inspired Lives."

VISIT OUR NEW SITE HOME AT
WWW.DESTINYIMAGE.COM

FREE SUBSCRIPTION TO DI NEWSLETTER

Receive free unpublished articles by top DI authors, exclusive
discounts, and free downloads from our best and newest books.
Visit www.destinyimage.com to subscribe.

Write to: Destiny Image
              P.O. Box 310
              Shippensburg, PA 17257-0310

Call: 1-800-722-6774

Email: orders@destinyimage.com

For a complete list of our titles or to place an order
online, visit www.destinyimage.com.